JOAN
OF THE EVERGLADES

D1251766

DAVID ATHEY

eLectio Publishing
Little Elm, TX
www.eLectioPublishing.com

Joan of the Everglades
By David Athey

Copyright 2017 by David Athey. All rights reserved.
Cover Design by eLectio Publishing.

ISBN-13: 978-1-63213-384-7

Published by eLectio Publishing, LLC
Little Elm, Texas
http://www.eLectioPublishing.com

Printed in the United States of America

5 4 3 2 1 eLP 21 20 19 18 17

The eLectio Publishing creative team is comprised of: Kaitlyn Campbell, Emily Certain, Lori Draft, Court Dudek, Jim Eccles, Sheldon James, and Christine LePorte.

Publisher's Note

Acknowledgments

Thank you, Beate Rodewald, for inspiring me to write a tale of "blood and thunder."

Thank you, Tom Chesnes, and Josh and Beka Holbrook, for driving me into the Everglades to search for giant pythons (and rattlesnakes, alligators, and other nightmarish things that appear in this book).

Thank you, Samantha Horkott and Chris Jensen, for reading the early versions and giving me great advice.

Thank you, Regina Doman and Andrew Schmiedicke, for your excellent insights.

Thank you, Olivia Anderson, for proofing this at Oxford University, offering brilliant feedback and not making a big deal about my ambivalence toward the Oxford comma.

Thank you, Savvy Myles, for making this novel a hundred times better.

Thank you, Stephanie Cassatly, for graciously suggesting eLectio Publishing.

Thank you, eLectio Team. You're the best.

Thank you, Kathleen Anderson, for always supporting my writing endeavors, no matter how ridiculous, even if that means my getting home from the Everglades in the middle of the night smelling of snakes and Skunk Ape. If that's not love, what is?

Introduction

Dear Reader, the heroine of this story, Joan Dior, was named after Joan of Arc, a mighty girl of the fifteenth century who helped France retain its royal independence. There are some parallels and unparallels between the medieval Joan and our modern Joan, and you might be inclined to gasp, laugh, lurch about in delirious fright, or guffaw loudly and declare: "This is utterly ridiculous! Whoever wrote this book ought to be burned at the stake!"

Yes, Dear Reader, all of those reactions are perfectly normal, especially when reading a story set in the Kingdom of Florida.

Chapter 1

The summer morning hissed with serpentine wisps of steam that slithered and died in the air between the salty waterway and fiery sky. Joan Dior and her best friend, Mia Kittinger, had recently graduated from high school and were drifting dead south in blood-red kayaks.

Joan had unwieldy tangles of purple hair that shrubbed around her dark eyes and proclaimed to the world: *Yes, I'm a bit dangerous; deal with it.* Her father was a soldier who died in Afghanistan, and so Joan coped by declaring war on everything that was not edgy and artistic. The girl was moody, sometimes blooming with bursts of energy, sometimes stark and prickly. Joan was not easy to hug, always wearing a camouflage T-shirt and combat boots, and don't even think about kissing her.

Mia was a freckled blonde with more brains than most of us. She'd led the debate team to a national title and was heading to Harvard in the fall. When asked if she'd be a political science major, Mia scoffed. "Major? Ha. Commander-in-Chief is more my style." And like most politicians, she liked nice clothes, and she loved being kissed.

The young women had attended Paradise School of the Arts, where Joan had nearly gotten expelled for painting the principal with the face of *The Scream*. Defending herself, she'd said, "Everyone feels like *The Scream* sometimes. The world is a very scary place."

"True," the principal replied. "And it's even scarier without a diploma."

Anyway, Joan managed to graduate and get accepted into the Savannah College of Art and Design, and now she was enjoying spending a summer day with Mia.

"I love being on the water," Joan said, observing the land from her kayak. She did not wear sunglasses, and she did not squint.

The shoreline was a mix of renovation, degradation, and wild beauty. A green parrot hovered on a power line between a mansion and a tiny cottage. "Be afraid," it squawked, "be not afraid."

"What did you say?" Joan asked.

The parrot paused, seemed to smile, and squawked again, "Be afraid. Be not afraid."

The explorers gaped at the parrot while they bobbed in the deep Intracoastal Waterway. "What a weird thing," Mia said. "Who trained it to say that? Two different people?"

Joan didn't answer, wondering why the green flame of a bird seemed to be staring straight into her soul. She felt there was more to the message, and waited for another phrase. Birds like that usually had a dozen or so messages to help human beings with their missions. Eventually, losing patience, Joan said, "Either say something more useful, or beat it!"

The parrot lurched and fell forward, still clinging to the power line, and spoke while swaying upside down. "Be afraid," it repeated. "Be not afraid."

Mia burst out laughing, rocking her kayak, while Joan wondered if the bird was a good or bad omen. "That's all, folks!" it said. "That's all, folks!"

Beneath the parrot was an overgrown garden that suggested the mansion was abandoned. Red grass rose like a fountain of blood while ghostly white orchids fluttered upon an avocado tree, making the tree seem otherworldly.

"C'mon," Mia urged, whacking the water with her paddle. "Let's keep going."

"Chill," Joan said, glaring at the strange bird and garden. "I need to paint this scene in my mind. Maybe I'll put it on canvas later."

Splashing her friend, Mia said, "If you don't start moving, you'll have to paint me as *The Scream*, because I will literally be screaming at you."

"Okay, okay. Let's go to the island."

"Be afraid," the upside-down parrot rasped, his words floating over their heads.

It was a fairly easy trip down to Apocalypse Island, with the current doing most of the work, tugging the kayaks across the easy blue, until a whale-sized yacht approached on huge rolling waves. The kayaks almost capsized, but Joan raised a paddle like a sword and yelled at the captain, "This is a manatee zone! Jerk!"

The skeletal-faced captain, grinning at the prow, steered the yacht toward the blazing ocean. "You stupid kids are lucky to be alive!"

Joan stood her ground on the water. She actually did stand on her kayak, performing a balancing act that only one in a thousand purple-haired girls can do, especially while wearing military boots. "You have to share the earth!" she yelled. "You don't own everything!"

Mia adjusted her large-brimmed hat and wiped some droplets from her sunglasses. "I think that yacht belongs to the WINGS."

"The what?"

"Wealth Initiative Networking Group for Society."

Joan glared at the yacht as it accelerated from the inlet into the ocean. The word WINGS on the hull, a sort of ugly dragon-red, made her feel especially edgy.

Changing the subject to something more handsome, Mia said, "I don't see Rico. He was supposed to meet us." She scanned the beach of Apocalypse Island. "Should I text him?"

"Kill the phone," Joan said, readjusting herself on the kayak. "We're supposed to be enjoying nature. If Rico's late like he usually is, you can swim for a while and I'll be your lifeguard."

"Swim? In a collared Polo? Not happening."

"Mia, aren't you wearing a swimsuit?"

"No, just skin underneath. Exfoliated, moisturized, and sun-blocked. Florida will never get the best of me."

"Yo, freckle face!" a young man shouted. "Yo!"

Rico's strong voice sang out from the inlet where he appeared like a sunrise god on the incoming tide. He'd already kayaked far out that morning, having braved the Gulf Stream while searching for sea monsters. Macabre creatures had recently washed up on beaches from Havana to Maine, the videos of the slimy leviathans going viral. Rico had wanted to catch a glimpse of a live one, and maybe drag the beastie to a research station, but the ocean had offered him no signs of monstrous life, not even a mid-sized turtle.

"He's not wearing a shirt," Joan said, not impressed. "He'd wear a shirt if he was serious about dating you."

Mia smiled, and perhaps stared at his abs.

"He's all yours," Joan said, hitting the shore. "Enjoy your non-date on Apocalypse Island."

"I don't care if it's a date or not," Mia said, sliding onto the sand. "It's educational. We're going on a tour of the Kennedy Bunker. It's not likely to be romantic."

"Anything to do with the Kennedys is romantic," Joan said, "and involves death. So be careful."

"I'll be careful," Mia answered, tilting her blonde head as if imparting wisdom through her floppy hat. "And you be cheerful. Smiling is good for your health."

Not quite smiling, Joan dragged the kayak to higher ground and dropped it with a thud and crunch upon a circle of shells. She waved goodbye over her shoulder and began marching inland, eager to visit the island's lagoon.

Waving her hat, Mia shouted, "Are you sure you don't want to see the Kennedy Bunker? Don't you care about underground history?"

Not looking back, Joan answered, "I'm good. Meet me at the lagoon when you get bored."

"What about the Cuban Missile Crisis? Don't you want to learn more about that?"

"Sorry. I'm not feeling like a crisis right now."

"So much for Joan," Rico said. His kayak nosed to shore and nudged Mia's. "Well, Freckles, looks like you'll have to handle the Cold War all by yourself."

"All by myself?" Mia tried to sound more inquisitive than hurt. "What's your plan?"

The young man leaned back in the kayak and turned his face toward the sun. "I'm gonna chill in the rays for a while."

Mia sighed. "Fine. Stay out here in the direct light and suffer the consequences of melanoma. According to the latest oncology study by the Florida Association of Dermatologists—"

"I welcome radiation," Rico said, closing his eyes. "I'm not afraid of being radiant. I'm not afraid of anything."

"What about your videos?"

He shrugged. "What videos?"

"Um, the hundred YouTube links you've sent? Secret societies, conspiracy theories, monsters. Paranoid much?"

Rico smiled, perfectly content, ready to fall into dreamland. "Oh yeah, *those* videos."

Mia smacked him with her hat. "This morning you started my day with *The Invisible Methane Monster*. Very cheery."

"Oh yeah," Rico said with a yawn. "If the Methane Monster arises from the Everglades, then we're all gonna die. But right now, I'm gonna chill on this beach."

Chapter 2

The ancient tour guide in the Kennedy Bunker stared at Mia with his one good eye, a yellowish orb that seemed ready to blink out, while his voice crackled like lightning. "JFK spent so much time at his estate on Palm Beach, it became known as 'The Winter White House.' So the military built this underground labyrinth here on Apocalypse Island in case war broke out during vacation time. President Kennedy had a red phone installed. A fire-red phone, for calling Castro or the big boys in Russia. Follow me around this corner and down to the War Room . . . down . . . down . . . follow me. Don't mind the darkness. It won't hurt you."

Joan was glad to be outside by herself, away from the tourists and military history. She knelt beside a glittering lagoon, her knees stinging on the rocks because of the rips in her black skinny jeans. She leaned over the still water, looking beyond her melancholy reflection in hopes of seeing exotic fish of many colors that would stir her soul. But the bottom of the lagoon was disappointing, awash in gray rocks and murky caverns.

"Where are the fish?" she murmured.

At the sound of her voice, there was a swirl of debris as if she'd spooked something. A mysterious creature flashed darkly in the underwater world, and disappeared.

Whispering to her reflection, Joan asked, "Was that a devil ray? Where did it go?"

"Don't ask me," the reflection answered. "This island is totally weird."

The artist raised her head and stared at the far side of the lagoon, where a colorful image graced the surface. It was something the size of a dolphin but all rainbow, like a kingfish, and crowned by seaweed. Joan stood and circled around, stumbling on pebbles and shells, trying to get a better look. When she reached the other end of the lagoon, she realized the colors were caused by an oil sheen.

"That's not good." Her stomach tensed. Had the latest oil spill snaked around the Keys and poisoned this side of paradise?

Images of death-slickened animals filled her head with a mix of sadness and horror. Breathing deep to fight the nausea, Joan leaned forward. *What on earth is that?*

Meanwhile, back inside the Bunker, crammed together with a dozen tourists, Mia raised her hand and asked, "Did President Kennedy ever use the red phone? Did he ever make an emergency call to Moscow?"

The one-eyed guide shuffled over to the presidential desk and picked up the scarlet receiver. "Hello, Mr. Ruskie? Are you listening? Well listen to this: your comrades will die! Ha ha, that's funny, I think. No, this phone is a cheap replacement. Nobody knows what happened to the original phone."

Most of the tourists seemed at a loss for words, but an elderly man from Iowa said, "I heard Marilyn Monroe stole it."

The guide squinted his sickly orb. "If the red phone had been dialed, it would have meant the nukes had been launched. It would have meant the slaughter of millions of innocent people. Listen, you are standing in one of the most dangerous places in all of history. You can feel the immensity of our mortality down here. This hole could have been the flashpoint of an actual Armageddon."

Those calamitous words made breathing difficult in a place already lacking in oxygen. The old Iowa man grew faint and leaned against the damp wall, gulping the foul air while Mia offered an arm of support and prepared to ask the guide about the intricacies of nuclear winter. Mia wanted to know if nuclear winter would be warmer and more bearable in Florida. And suddenly there was a scream, a terrified cry from the sunlit world, descending down the twisting, serpentine tunnel, filling the War Room with echoes of the scream, over and over again.

Chapter 3

Dear Reader, we must leave behind a corpse on Apocalypse Island and think good thoughts for Joan and Mia (there is a fifty-percent chance they will survive) while we venture forth to a dank, dark cathedral. Actually, the cathedral smells like oranges and is very bright. It doesn't even have gargoyles or a secret crypt full of medieval mystical bones. Man, what has happened to cathedrals?

Anyway, if you're averse to discussions of things like exorcisms and oil spills, then you may want to skip a few chapters.

Chapter 4

The cathedral bells did not toll, but rather chimed like a steel-drum melody at nine in the morning. Two men in shiny black clothes waited until the silence returned. "As I was saying," the bishop said, leaning forward over his ornate desk, "when the man from British Petroleum called at midnight, he said, 'I have bloodied myself, and I have bloodied others.'"

Father Pierre, a Haitian scholar, pretended to stick his fingers in his ears. "Please, do not reveal the confession. You know the rules, boss."

"Listen. We have to figure out what he meant by that talk of blood."

"I should not know about that secret confession."

"But it was not a confession," the bishop said, his voice trembling. "It was something much worse. It was a boast."

Chapter 5

Dressed in a gray suit and fedora, the Brit slithered into the cathedral's main office as if nobody would question him, but was suddenly stopped by the office manager, Mrs. Teffler. Thinking he was a salesman, she coolly asked, "Have you been summoned?"

The visitor smirked. "Summoned? Summoned by a summoner?"

Mrs. Teffler scowled and cleared her throat. "Do you have an appointment?"

The man in gray smiled charmingly. "Yes, indeed, my sweet. We've had an appointment for a thousand years. Now please let us in."

"Us?"

"Yes. We are British Petroleum."

Mrs. Teffler had dealt with every type of person under the sun, individuals with every sort of spiritual and emotional problem, and this was the first time in twenty years that she felt the urge to squirt a bottle of holy water at the face of a visitor.

Reaching into her desk for the bottle, she said, "Whom shall I say is calling?"

The man and his fedora towered over her, his cold eyes boring down. "Tell him the whole world is calling."

Before Mrs. Teffler could relay the message, the Brit slithered into the bishop's study, curled up on a chair, and began chatting as if they were old friends.

"My dear bishop, you know how I love Florida. There is nothing like a man-made paradise, and I must sing hosanna to the Breakers Hotel. The staff treats me like royalty. In fact, last night there was a knock at my door—I was watching the moonlit ocean and searching for slick colors on the water—and Room Service appeared, offering me a bowl of strawberries and goat yogurt."

"How nice," the bishop replied, "now tell me—"

"Yes, yes," the visitor said, adjusting his hat to make it crooked. "I have been served like a prince at the Breakers. No matter the little mess BP made in the Gulf. Did you see all the floating fishes and birds? Have you ever seen anything so dead and pretty?"

The bishop stared deeply into the man's eyes, trying to discern the activity of his soul, and asked, "How can I help you?"

"Well, I'm glad you asked, my middle-aged chap. May I have a serving of mangoes with ice cream? With Cuban coffee? And could I trouble you, please, to serve it in a magic cauldron?"

"Excuse me?"

"I'll excuse you to the kitchen."

Glancing at his daily calendar, the bishop wiped sweat from his eyes and said, "Forgive me, but I have a busy schedule today. I will say goodbye now."

The visitor frowned. "Say it isn't so. A thousand times no. You cannot send me away yet. We have not descended to our business."

"Our business?"

"Yes, we spoke through the airwaves yesterday about our secret business. The blood."

The bishop whispered, "You sound like an actor." And he really hoped that was the case.

"Indeed," the Brit said. "There are actors crawling within my skin, and they perform all sorts of things. One of them plays a murderer. Another one plays a murderer. And two of them are worse than that."

"Seriously, are you having trouble distinguishing real life from drama? Because it seems like you're play-acting."

The man rolled his eyes. "Don't you know anything? According to the shaker of the spear, 'All the world's a stage.' Shaker knew the real Globe Theatre is the human soul, the ultimate stage for tragedies."

"And comedies as well?" The bishop had seen TV shows in which practical jokes were played out on unsuspecting victims.

Perhaps the Brit had a hidden camera and was recording their meeting to disseminate publicly—to make the church look bad.

"Thank you for visiting. Good day, sir. Goodbye."

The stranger curled deeper into the chair. He grinned, laughed, and began to convulse and groan. His eyes became sickly white and rolled to the back of his head.

"Stop that," the bishop said, looking for signs of a camera or other recording device. There was something in the man's jacket, but it might have been a wallet. Or was it a gun?

Bursting through the door, the Haitian appeared, his black robe fluttering as if he'd been carried by the wind. "Hello, boss. How are you?"

"Well, um, I seem to have a problem with British Petroleum." He gestured toward the convulsing man. "Or with some practical joker."

The young scholar ambled toward the visitor, offering a warm smile. Instantly the man blinked his eyes and became himself again. He whirled in his chair. "Did you bring the apricots and tea? Have you been sent from Room Service?"

"Hello. I am Pierre."

"Hello. I am the Prince of Wales."

"That is quite the joke," Father Pierre said with a gracious smile. He circled the bizarre man, whispered a prayer in Creole, and gently placed his hand beneath the brim of the fedora. "You have the fever," he said, removing his hand and making the sign of the Cross. "I have known the fever in my country."

The stranger pulled his hat down tightly around his head. "Do you want a donation or not? There are other powers in Florida. We could give this check to them." He reached into a gray pocket and fished out an oily piece of paper. "It is a substantial gift," the Brit said, "to make us consubstantial."

"You must be the one to leave," the Haitian said. "You must go and take the aspirin."

"But . . ."

"Aspirin. Take at least two."

A smirk crossed the stranger's face. He stood tall again. "Indeed. We shall return to our castle and swallow thirteen aspirin. And our head will swim in ecstasy, like a mango in a magic cauldron. And we shall call again."

"We offer the blessings," Father Pierre said, bowing.

The Brit reached out and dropped the soiled check on the bishop's desk. "Now let us shakes on it."

"Shakes on what? Did we make an agreement?"

"Yes. I promise not to bloody anyone until we meet again."

The bishop paused and then shook hands, only for a second, and the Brit immediately slithered out of the room. He blew a kiss at Mrs. Teffler, who huffed at him from behind her desk and aimed a bottle of holy water. "Don't make me blast you," she said. A few moments later, she called out, "The coast is clear. He's gone."

"Ugh, I need to clean my hand," the bishop said.

Mrs. Teffler brought him a box of sanitary wipes. "Do you believe he's really a BP executive?"

The bishop tried to remove the oily smudge. "I don't know what he is."

"What a weirdo," Mrs. Teffler said. "Good riddance. Now we can get on with the day."

The young scholar stared out the window. "But they are coming back."

The bishop raised an eyebrow. "They?"

"Yes, boss. There were several in his eyes."

"He wasn't faking it?"

"He is the one for faking, yes, and he is the one for possessing, too. Sadly, he does not want to be healed." Father Pierre closed the blinds and stood staring at the fractured light resonating between the cracks. "Spiritual discernment is everything, boss, and you must make the right decision."

Mrs. Teffler cut in. "I told the bishop to appoint a new exorcist. I told the bishop that he didn't need this sort of pressure. I told him—"

"Thank you, Teresa," the bishop said, dripping with perspiration. "You were right. You can return to your desk now."

Mrs. Teffler stomped away. "I don't enjoy being right all the time. I'm just trying to help around here."

"Thank you, Teresa."

"Yeah, yeah," she muttered. "I'll just sit at my desk and say sweet little prayers all day."

"That would be helpful," the bishop said.

"Boss?"

"Yes, Pierre?"

The Haitian turned from the window. "The war is upon us. And you will need the reinforcements."

Chapter 6

Dear Reader, although the previous chapters contained some *foreshadowing* (a term employed by the literati to mean "shadowing at the fore") you didn't really miss anything by skipping those pages.

Except . . . there was a kissing scene. And this is a "kissing book," after all. However, the kiss was merely one of those fake smacks (for which Brits are famous) and the smacker was a demon-possessed executive from British Petroleum who has a thing for ecclesiastical secretaries. I think we can properly surmise that he will get blasted by holy water.

Now then, let us hope Joan and Mia, our mighty but mortal heroines, are still alive. And let us hope they will never be kissed, like so many nice girls are, by blathering idiots.

Okay, onward to the next chapter. This one should not be skipped—because of a dead body, and you get to meet a French giant.

Chapter 7

Joan screamed again. Leaning over the murky edge of the lagoon, she screamed at the sight of a dead girl floating in the water, then turned and ran in a panic to where Rico was sleeping soundly on his kayak. "Rico! Rico! Call the police!"

He flinched awake. "Huh? What?"

"Call the police!"

"Really?"

"Yes!"

Rico dialed 911 and handed her the phone. "What's going on? Is Mia okay?"

The operator asked Joan to state the nature of her emergency.

"My emergency," Joan said, gasping, "is death. I'm reporting a death! There's a dead girl on Apocalypse Island—in the lagoon by the underground bunker."

The operator inquired if the female was definitely deceased.

"Yes, I'm sure!"

Rico's face went ashen. "Is Mia okay?"

"She's floating face-up in the water," Joan told the operator. "You want a description of the body? She was covered with oil and seaweed. She looked like a teenager. She had a sad face. What? Yes, she was wounded. I don't think she drowned. I think she was stabbed."

Rico lunged out of the kayak. "What's going on? Tell me where Mia is!"

"She's okay, Rico. She's down in the bunker. She's safe."

"I'm going to find her!"

"What, operator? Yes, I can wait near the body. Yes, I promise. I won't let anyone touch her."

Sirens blared on both the mainland and the waterway. Within a few minutes, various boats with flashing lights roared up to the dock and beach, including a Coast Guard unit, a police boat, and an EMT. Professionals in uniforms scrambled to shore and scurried toward the lagoon while Rico and Mia stood in the shade of a tiki hut, watching with worried faces as Joan directed the first responders to where the girl was floating. "She's right over here! But not everyone should look. She doesn't have any clothes on."

Flash, flash—photographs were taken from every angle, and then a Coast Guard officer waded into the water, put on plastic gloves, and carefully grasped the girl's foot.

At that moment, Joan began to weep. She stood in the sunshine, her purple hair fluttering in the breeze like a painting of despair. She wept as quietly as possible, her back to the photographers, until a big bald detective placed a large hand on her shoulder. "I need to ask you some questions." He was sort of pushy while escorting Joan across the sand toward the tiki hut where the other teenagers stood waiting. Mia stepped out of the shelter, her words like a hug. "Are you okay? Here, take these." Mia removed her large sunglasses and placed them on Joan, knowing that her friend hated for people to see her cry.

The bald detective pulled out his phone, aimed it at Rico, and began asking him questions about everything that had happened that morning. Being recorded made Rico nervous and he stammered, "I don't know—anything about that dead chick. You need to ask Joan. She's the one who found her."

"Thank you for your cooperation," the detective said, and then he peppered all three teenagers with questions they couldn't answer, including:

How long has the girl been dead?

What is that tattoo on her thigh?

Did she visit the island often?

Did the girl come here at night?

Was she a good dancer?

"I don't know," was the echoed response.

After thirty minutes of questioning, the teens were finally left alone. The corpse was placed in a body bag and taken away in a boat that seemed to roar toward the ocean instead of toward land.

The three friends stood together in the shade of the tiki hut, not speaking, until several more minutes passed and Rico finally said, "Let's get out of here."

Mia nodded. "We should call for a water taxi. I don't want to kayak in this heat. Does that sound like a good idea, Joan? Should we call a taxi?"

"No, not yet." Joan turned and stared at some scraggly pine trees, the last pines remaining that hadn't been replaced by palms. "I think something weird is about to happen."

That was a strange phrase, considering that something weird had already happened. Rico and Mia said nothing but gave each other concerned looks.

"Something weird is about to happen," Joan repeated.

However, nothing happened, except the sun rose higher and the trees became brighter, an east wind roared from the ocean, and a seabird screeched a lonely note. And then, in a sudden calm, the trees seemed to become all fire.

And then it happened.

A French giant appeared.

Perhaps because of Joan's tears, refracting and intensifying her vision, the giant seemed to appear through a fiery doorway of unburned branches. Joan removed the borrowed sunglasses and squinted. And she squinted again, because the giant seemed to be suffused, diffused, and completely fused with a strange power and a weird glory. And she was the only one who saw him. The brown-robed giant could have been named Andre but was actually known as "Brother Bean" because in the fifteenth century a wandering mystic had helped Joan of Arc find beans for her army.

"I greet you, my joy," the giant said, striding on bare feet toward the tiki hut.

And I greet you, Joan thought. *Can I help you?*

"I am at your service," he replied. Brother Bean bowed to Joan and gently brushed away the last of her tears.

"My joy," he said, straightening up to his full height. "The days of doom are upon us. You must be brave, and say your prayers, and resist all evil. These lands are under occupation by visible and invisible forces. I will try to guard you in this war, but I cannot save you from your own heart. Let all of your thoughts be heavenly."

And with that, the brown-robed giant turned and padded away until he disappeared into the doorway among the shimmering, scraggly pines.

Chapter 8

Dear Reader, have you ever had a day like that? If so, you probably need to put this book down and seek professional help. Or maybe you are the professional help. If so, then why don't you help us?

Chapter 9

A retired exorcist lived in a historic area of West Palm Beach called Old Northwood. Between the wealthy shoreline and some ruins near the railroad tracks, Father Adam was like a hermit in a musty, tin-roofed cottage surrounded by a jungle of tropical trees, shrubs, and flowering weeds. The neighbors referred to his place as "Eden's Hellhole" and were always calling the weed inspector, demanding enforcement of the rules. However, the inspector allowed the yard to grow wild because the cottage seemed like a quaint painting, and the priest's three prowling cats helped to control the creepy-crawly things in the neighborhood, including spiders, rats, snakes, and scorpions.

The old exorcist was crowned by a ring of thinning white hair, and his face was spiked with sparse whiskers, as if handfuls had been plucked out in fights. He wore a faded purple bowling shirt and khaki pants stained with an assortment of soups he spilled while spluttering at the television. He'd become known as Father Cranky Pants, not because of his stained khakis, but because he was angry about the clothes (or lack thereof) that he saw on TV. The priest was especially disturbed by the antics of Lady Myras, who seemed to be on every channel, day and night, twerking.

The exorcist tried to be merciful, coughing cigarette smoke at the screen while mumbling the prayer of absolution for the twerking Lady Myras—"*Et ego te absolvo a peccatis tuis in nomine Patris, et Filii, et Spiritus Sancti.* NOW STOP DOING THAT!"

Click.

Knock knock.

Saturday afternoon, there was somebody at the door of the cottage. The exorcist snuffed out his cigarette, finished his prayer, and limped across the living room. "Who's there?"

No answer.

"I won't buy anything."

No answer.

"And I won't join your cult."

The knocking grew louder.

"For the love of . . ."

Father Adam opened the creaking door, expecting some minor irritation or major curse. And he was greeted by a smiling Haitian.

"I am Pierre."

"I know. Go away."

"Please listen. The boss sends a dozen regards. And he needs your help."

The old man scoffed and slammed the door.

Knock, knock. "I am Pierre, still here."

"Go away! Don't you understand English?"

Knock, knock. "I am the one who understands many languages."

"Yes, I know about the books you've published. Well done. But go away! I'm retired. And I'm exhausted. Lady Myras is killing me."

"Please. We are saying the *please*."

"Oh, for crap's sake. Do you think you can wear me down with politeness?"

"Yes. I will keep on saying the *please* all day."

"Oh, for . . ." Against his will, Father Adam opened the door. "Listen to me, young man. Some day you'll be an old priest, like me, with bad teeth and inflamed joints and brains full of fuzzy mush, and—"

The Haitian laughed.

The laugh was so full of innocence and mirth that the exorcist could not resist joining in. His own laugh was like a rattling death gasp, and it almost choked him. "Oh, crap," he coughed. "James really wants me to return, huh?"

Father Pierre nodded. "You are the man."

The elder cleric pulled a pack of cigarettes from his pocket and lit one up, inhaling with all his strength. "I'm nothing but a dead man."

"Dead or alive, you must battle the devils."

"Seriously? You've got to be joking." The exorcist blew smoke toward the floor and watched it swirl upward. He could sense a new infestation of dark energy in the world, but he thought his fighting days, at least regarding official church work, were over. The battle would have to be won by other warriors.

Chapter 10

Joan's mom knocked softly on the bedroom door. "Are you okay in there, honey? Are you hungry? I made some toast for you."

"I'm okay," the girl said. She lay slumped on the bed in her black pajamas.

"Are you sure? Can you try a piece of toast?"

"Maybe later."

Joan's mom hovered at the door. She was a nurse and knew full well that her daughter was suffering from the trauma of finding a dead body. She wanted Joan to speak with a counselor, but she knew Joan wouldn't agree to that. Joan always dealt with everything in her own mysterious way.

"I'll leave the toast outside the door."

"Okay, but I'll probably go to sleep early."

"All right. Well, the food is here if you need it. Goodnight, Joanie."

"Night, Mom."

Joan brushed the bruise-colored locks from her eyes and stared at the art poster in the center of the wall. She'd put *The Scream* there after her father was killed and after her mom talked about the five stages of grief and how she'd get through them and eventually be okay. But Joan didn't want to be okay with death. She wanted death to die.

"I don't know why that girl was murdered," she whispered to *The Scream*, "but I'm going to find out. I'm taking a vow. I will find the killer."

Joan kept focused on the poster for several more minutes, thinking about her dad and how so many families were suffering from loss and loneliness, and then the image on the wall disappeared, because something—or somebody—seemed to be standing between her and *The Scream*. Joan blinked, and the shape became clear and bright, but not as tall or strange as a French giant, because the visitor in her room was a medium-sized angel.

"You have vowed to solve the murder," the angel said, his voice both serene and powerful. "That is a very terrible vow, placing you in the center of battle."

"What!"

Joan had barely gasped the word when the angel vanished and *The Scream* reappeared.

The girl could have convinced herself that nothing had happened, that she hadn't really seen an angel and heard a voice, because two visions on the same day were, perhaps, a bit much. But Joan, being artsy and soulful, was not someone who eschewed celestial visitations. "Whoa," she murmured. "That was real. Whoa. Time to get to work." She jumped out of bed, hurried to the desk, and fired up her father's old computer. After a deep breath and a quick prayer, she began doing research. "What's her name? What's her name?" she whispered to the screen while typing "apocalypse island corpse lagoon." Instantly, the tragedy appeared on Twitter, with multiple theories about how the girl was murdered.

"Or a suicide," someone commented. *"Her name is Donna Murskey. She lived on Palm Beach when she wasn't at boarding school. She was known in drug circles."*

Donna Murskey . . .

The name had a familiar ring, but Joan wasn't sure if she'd ever met the girl. Maybe at a coffee shop? Joan grabbed her phone and called Mia. "Hey, do you know someone from Palm Beach named—"

"Donna Murskey."

"You already know?"

"Yeah. It's been out for an hour. Dontey was in the loop, and he called Rico, and then Rico texted me, and—"

"And nobody told me? I'm the one in the middle of this whole thing. I'm the one who looked into Donna's face and saw my reflection. I'm the one who just got visited . . . by a . . ."

"I'm sorry, Joan. We thought you already knew. We thought some official would have told you."

Joan rubbed a wrinkle on her pajamas, one of the many frowns in the fabric that wouldn't go away. "Nobody told me anything."

"We didn't want to bother you. We thought you'd want to be alone."

"Well, you were right. I wanted to be alone. But you were wrong, too."

Mia felt terrible for being both right and wrong. She always wanted to be right, especially when it came to her best friend. "I'm really sorry, Joan. Good thing you and I have always been fast forgivers. Don't be mad for long, okay?"

Staring again at the wall and *The Scream*, Joan thought about the angel and the giant, and how their faces were gentle. Even while speaking of battle, their demeanor was all peaceful. "I'll forgive you, Mia. If . . ."

"If what?"

"You tell me everything you know about Donna Murskey."

"I don't know much about her, except, well, she was beautiful and edgy. Like you, Joan."

Those words almost brought out tears, but Joan blinked them away. She didn't want to think about being beautiful and edgy. She wanted to do something beautiful and edgy—and dangerous. She wanted to solve the mystery of who murdered Donna.

Chapter 11

Donna Joy Murskey had the dual existence of the typical Palm Beach girl, raised to be completely isolated from the ordinary world, and yet overly exposed to the worldly. Her family lived on the north end of the island, between the old Kennedy compound and the new Limbaugh compound. Donna's bedroom had a lovely view of the ocean, but her boarding schools were landlocked—cold, dark places in Vermont and upstate New York. She hated being away from the tropical lushness of Florida, and she always fell into severe depressions.

Donna's parents, like most parents on Palm Beach, tried to mold their daughter into a perfect socialite, although nobody knew what the perfect socialite actually was. Republican? Democrat? Curvy? Anorexic? Save the whales? Save the manatees? Eat turtle soup? Should the perfect socialite show off the diamonds and gold or hide them in Zurich? Drink the best elixirs of booze or buy a clinic of happy pills?

Donna's head, when it wasn't spinning, felt like it was deep underwater.

And to make matters worse, at the age of fifteen, the dark-skinned beauty was enlisted as a dancer for a major social event. Along with several other Palm Beach girls, Donna was told to dress in a trampy outfit and dance in a garden for the WINGS.

The night before the rehearsal, Donna pouted at the family dining table and muttered, "I don't want to be in the show."

"Oh, the dance will be delightful," her mother snapped as politely as possible. "Glabdina is doing the choreography."

Donna's father glanced up from his herb-encrusted sea bass. "Who's doing the choreography?"

"Tinsel Glabdina. She did *Polanski in Chains* last year on Broadway."

Mr. Murskey rolled his eyes. "How did I miss that?"

"Why, you were in Bali, dear. I went to *Polanski in Chains* with Moppet. Remember? I stayed for a week at Moppet's Cape Cod in the Hamptons."

Mr. Murskey picked at his crusty bass. "It's dry as hell. How many times must I tell the chef to lower the heat? He likes to watch those infernal cooking shows and dance around the flames."

Mrs. Murskey smiled with a frown. "The fish is fine."

"No," Mr. Murskey said, pushing the plate away. "The big-screen television is coming out of the kitchen. I knew it was a mistake."

Donna, who hadn't eaten a thing, said, "May I be excused?"

"No, dear," her mother said. "You will need a good mix of proteins and carbohydrates for the dance rehearsal. Imagine! You will be working with a Broadway savant."

"More like an idiot savant."

"What did you say, dear?"

The girl slouched away from the table. "Nothing, Mother."

Mr. Murskey glared at his perfectly made-up wife. "Are you sure Donna needs to perform at that event?"

"I'm sure. The performance will be a splendid experience for our daughter. In fact, it will be life-changing. Absolutely life-changing."

Although Donna hated moving her body for the delight of old men's eyes, she obeyed her mother and danced for the WINGS at their October fundraiser. The *Demon Dance* was an open celebration of all things hellish in a garden of earthly atrocities, the decorations consisting of lights in the form of blood droplets, severed baby skulls dangling on coconut trees, and upside-down crosses circling a red swimming pool near a macabre, spider-webbed stage where children dirty-danced for charity.

Donna almost threw up in the middle of it, but forced herself to smile and be professional. After the performance, she stood near a fountain that was oozing blackness. Away from the other dancers, she was trying to catch her breath, and crying a little, when a man in a scarlet mask approached her. "Lovely little Donna Joy. I remember you as a pixie tramping down the aisle at the Boar's Head Festival."

"Oh, yeah," she said, glancing away. "I hated that show."

The man in the mask slid around to meet her gaze. "You were the star of the Boar's Head. You sparkled like sweetness itself in the church. And tonight, in the garden, you were an absolute goddess."

Donna laughed nervously and adjusted her flesh-colored outfit. "Well, at least at this show I didn't have to dance with a candle in my hand and get burned."

The masked man nodded as if understanding her every struggle and concern. "You had to work hard as a child to achieve artistic perfection. And what a divine adult you've become."

"Adult? Tell that to my parents."

"I know your parents very well. But they barely know me."

Donna sighed. "I like to keep them in the dark as much as I can."

The man reached out and touched the girl's face. He seemed to have something cosmic inside his flesh. "Do you believe," he said, "in this world of the blind and lame? Or do you believe in a secret world of strength and light?"

"A secret world?"

"Of strength and light. Do you know it?"

Searching for signs of color in the masked man's eyes, the girl said, "I'd like to know more about that world."

There was a flash of teeth. "I'll bring you to a place where there is nothing, nothing except the darkness of beautiful light, a place where nothing seems like anything, where everything *IS*."

The girl moved toward the black fountain. "I'm sort of busy this week."

"Ah, well. There is a gathering next Sunday. All the men of strength and light would love to meet you. And they will adore you."

Adore? The word made Donna smirk, it was so absurd. And yet there was something so alluring about being the object of adoration. She'd been *liked* by some boys, and there was one who would have *loved* her, had circumstances allowed, but to be *adored*? Wasn't that a word reserved for immortals? And now this rich and powerful man in a mask was making her feel, even with some guilt, like she was immortal.

Chapter 12

The bishop sat slumped behind his desk, sweating and rubbing his temples. "I've been thinking, and I believe I have a good idea."

The young scholar nodded. "Good ideas are the good ones, boss."

"Listen, Pierre. I need you to gather an official committee. The Spiritual Warfare Committee. I want you to lead the battle against, well, whatever we're up against."

The guileless Haitian put on a brave face. "I am not the strong one, but I will help."

The bishop smiled weakly. "You're the strongest person I know."

"I am not so great. But I will gather the warriors. I am sorry about Adam not joining us. He is the cranky one."

"Yes, very cranky."

"And I will try to find the woman who lives in the wilderness that could kill me."

"I appreciate your attitude." The bishop leaned forward in his chair and rubbed his sore temples. After a long minute, he said, "Pierre, I have some terrible news."

"Is it very terrible?"

"Yes, it is. A reporter from the *Palm Beach Post* called me and said that a girl was recently murdered."

"A local girl?"

"Yes. The victim's name is Donna Murskey. Her parents are members at St. Edward's, and Donna was their only child."

Tears welled up in the Haitian's eyes.

The bishop looked down at his desk. "The girl was seventeen. And she was pregnant."

"Her baby," Father Pierre said, pausing for a moment before daring to ask, "is among the living?"

"I'm sorry to upset you with these words, but Donna's baby was ripped from the womb and not found at the scene. The reporter said it appears to be a ritual slaying, a cult sacrifice."

31

Chapter 13

The ocean was a blue fire. A few clouds bubbled up on the horizon, but no rain fell upon the boiling water. Rico and Dontey, shirtless and wearing swim trunks, were on the shore tossing a football, throwing it high and leaping toward the surf to make spectacular catches, while a group of female sunbathers from Scandinavia, burning on white towels, clapped their hands whenever one of the guys—especially Dontey, who actually was a football star—flew into the waves.

A voice called down from the lifeguard tower: "Pardon me, you gentlemen with the football. Please come up here."

Rico and Dontey, seeing the detective in the sky, wanted to make a run for it, but a patrol car was parked near the seawall, and there was no escape from Palm Beach. The drawbridges could be lifted at any moment, keeping any suspects from fleeing to the mainland.

"Better do what the man says," Dontey said. He was the son of a famous black minister and always felt extra pressure to stay out of trouble.

"We could hide," Rico whispered. He pointed north toward Clarke Beach and its cluster of sea grape bushes. "We could hide until sunset, and then—"

The detective interrupted. "Don't make me hunt you down. Now come up here. I need to have a few words with you boys. Mostly with you, Ricardo."

"Only my dad calls me that," Rico said. "And only when I'm in real trouble."

Dontey and Rico climbed the hot, sand-covered stairs of the lifeguard tower and entered the stifling room. The detective, wearing a white raincoat, was the same guy who'd questioned them on Apocalypse Island. He shook their hands and squeezed hard to test their strength, first the football star, and then the future soldier. "Good. You're both quite strong." He plopped down on a chair, sweat pouring from his puffy red face. "My name is Beauchamp.

Now, tell me the truth. Do you boys know anything—anything at all—about the murder of Donna Murskey?"

"No, sir," Dontey said, looking the detective straight in the eyes.

"Nope," Rico said, glancing out the door.

Beauchamp played with his thin moustache that resembled a line of dark sweat above his lip. "Hmm. The newspaper quoted an anonymous source, saying that Donna was involved in the local drug scene. Did you boys know she was into drugs?"

"I never met her," Dontey said.

"I don't know anything," Rico said, slowly making a fist.

The detective stood and flashed his badge. Even in the shade of the lifeguard tower, it was bright enough to make the guys blink. "You. Out," he said only to Dontey.

"Okay, sir." And Dontey was down the stairs in three leaps.

Rico made a move to follow his friend, but was stopped immediately by the sweaty inquisitor. "Sit down in that chair, Ricardo. And start telling me the truth."

Hesitating, and then deciding to obey, Rico sat and stared at the floor. "I've done nothing wrong. At least nothing wrong that has anything to do with Donna's death."

Beauchamp put his meaty hand on the young man's shoulder. "You knew her, though, didn't you?"

"Well. Sort of."

"Sort of, meaning you saw the girl at a party? Sort of, meaning you flirted with her? Or sort of, meaning you left the party with Donna Murskey and had relations with her on the beach? And maybe, sort of, got her pregnant?"

Chapter 14

Mother Heron was a beautiful old Seminole who lived in a log cabin overlooking the Loxahatchee River. She was the only person allowed to have a home in the nature preserve, having defeated the authorities in what became known as the "Seminole War of 1977."

Banishing one lone Indian from the riverside should have been easy for the government, but the *Palm Beach Post* sent a reporter to the wilderness, a young man fresh out of college who took an award-winning photo of the woman warrior making a peaceful protest. Mother Heron was floating on her back in the river among the hungry alligators, her face just inches from the jaws of a monster. The newspaper headline said: FEEDING TIME FOR BUREAUCRACY.

A groundswell of support for Mother Heron caused the bureaucrats to get creative with the rules of the wilderness preserve. They "grandfathered in" the grandmother, and she became the mystic guardian of the lovely, deadly river.

Father Pierre, on the other hand, had a phobia of wild water, knowing the stories of many people who had capsized and drowned while journeying from Haiti to Florida. But when the bishop asked him to brave the river and recruit Mother Heron for the Spiritual Warfare Committee, he agreed to the quest, saying, "In my weakness, the Lord is the strong one. And I have the good map."

Chapter 15

"I hope Mother finds me," Father Pierre murmured, utterly lost in the wilderness and wobbling on a blood-colored kayak. "This map is the worthless one."

A large water moccasin, just a few feet away, slithered aggressively over the surface of the river on its morning hunt. The creature lifted its neck to claim its territory, fangs glistening like tiny angels of death while the Haitian hummed a joyful hymn and tried to pretend that the venomous serpent did not exist.

"It is only a twig," he told himself. "The twig is a hissing one."

The deadly snake wriggled toward shore, and Father Pierre allowed the current to drag him downstream and deeper into the prehistoric jungle. Giant ferns and cypress trees lined both sides of the river like mythological armies. Birds cried out, and cried again, while the priest maneuvered through branches, petrified stumps, and floating logs that were covered with scales. The floating logs blinked their eyes, then sunk beneath the surface.

The twisting, turning Loxahatchee was ever-changing in width and the speed of its current. Pierre tried to stay in the middle, away from the muddy shore and its spiders, lizards, poisonous plants, wild boars, snakes, sinkholes, and more alligators. The Haitian was now in Real Florida, a place full of wrong turns and dangerous dead ends, and he had to sometimes paddle backward, splashing around in one of the backwaters, because an aggressive log opened its mouth, showing its teeth.

"Those are not teeth. Those are . . . something else."

A frantic hour passed before Father Pierre felt somewhat at ease, focusing on the bright flashes of fish and colorful wings of birds—when he saw a tin-roofed cabin set back among a clearing. Wisps of smoke drifted out of the chimney, smelling of some kind of delicious bread. Gracing the front door was a mosaic of shimmering beads.

"This is the place," the young scholar declared, nodding. "This is the place like a book."

He made a sharp turn and caused the front of the kayak to land on shore, but the rest of the craft was still in the water, being pummeled by the current. Attempting to stand, the nervous priest wobbled, his paddle flailing wildly, droplets flashing in slashing light . . . and then Father Pierre fell overboard, breathless, splashing into the river and drifting into the open jaws of a giant alligator.

Chapter 16

The barista at Bullion Coffee on Palm Beach liked Mia's fashion sense, but she narrowed her eyes at Joan's camo shirt. "Here are your drinks, um, *ladies*."

Joan grabbed her black coffee and stomped away, followed by Mia, who now wished she'd left a smaller tip. The young women took their drinks and sat near the glass-encased waterfall, which was almost silent, so they could hear if people were talking about Donna Murskey. If anyone knew important secrets, it would be the regulars on Worth Avenue.

Two swarthy men, both named Jake, guzzled at their usual table where they complained about waste management. Seated across from them, at a larger table, was a very sophisticated older couple, the man drinking Japanese tea and his wife sipping chai. Further back in the room was a handsome young man staring at his phone, apparently not paying attention to anything else while fashionistas in line bombarded the barista with questions, exclamations, and orders: "Did you see the big story in the news? Death is so awful! Skinny venti caramel mocha double-dolphin-dare Fountain of Youth with an extra shot!"

The semi-judgmental barista tried to keep up with the drinks and chatter, responding, "Yes, the druggie Murskey girl. What a terrible tragedy. Would you like a sample of our new seaweed cracker bites with your double-dolphin dare?"

The customers sampled and guzzled and talked about shopping, waste management, and death while Joan and Mia sat in the comfy chairs, eavesdropping on the wealth of gossip. Every once in a while, Joan got up to wander around, pretending to read info on the bulletin board or feigning interest in the flashy magazines in the dark bookcase. She overheard the Two Jakes discussing the layout of the Murskey mansion and the secret location of the recycling bins; and she overheard the elderly couple lamenting an article in *The Wall Street Journal*.

The gentleman was actually flummoxed by the story and beginning to perspire. He reached into the pocket of his navy blazer and grabbed a gold-embroidered handkerchief to mop his unruly eyebrows. "How dare they? How dare a lobbyist group for a shadow corporation try to make real life illegal? This makes me so flummoxed, even my eyebrows are perspiring."

His wife, wearing a power pink summer dress, replied with a sophisticated, "Yikes."

"Indeed. They are lobbying for legislation—in every country—to make GMO food the only legal food; and to make cloned animals the only ones on earth; and to make transhumanism mandatory. Each person, by law, will have their flesh computerized and on the grid."

The lady wished her husband would stop reading the news. She sipped her chai and chose her words carefully. "If I were Queen of the World, everything would be organic and free range. Including you, Gregory."

After listening to that intriguing conversation, Joan meandered toward the back of the coffee shop, where she was drawn to the handsome guy in the corner. He had a look reminiscent of her father. Dressed in a dark green suit, he seemed to be a veteran, with his hair grown out like tangled raven wings. The man looked up and smiled, his eyes mesmerizing, and he gave Joan a knowing nod. She was uneasy about starting a conversation with a guy who seemed almost thirty, but she felt compelled to ask, "Did you know her?"

"Did I know her?" he echoed. The handsome man spoke slowly, with a neo-Slavic accent almost as thick as his hair. "Of whom do you speak?"

"Donna Murskey."

"Oh, Donna." He rubbed at a smiling wrinkle on his green suit. "Why do you ask?"

Reluctant, yet brave because of her vow, Joan sat in the chair facing him. She placed her folded hands on the table and said with great effort, "I discovered the body."

"On Apocalypse Island," he said.

"Yeah."

Handsome began typing on his phone. *"Discovered the body."* He looked up. "And your name is—"

"Joan."

"Yes. Joan Dior," the man said. "And your phone number?"

"I don't think so, dude."

"Well then, never mind," he said. "All in good time."

"You think?" Joan raised her arm and invited Mia to the table. "Mia. Hey! Over here."

Mia waved back but stayed in her chair, ensconced in a conversation with a bright and shiny jeweler.

"I don't give out my number," Joan said in a prickly voice. "Not to strangers."

"I'm not a stranger," Handsome said.

"Well, I don't know who you are."

"Actually, you do."

"How?"

"Facebook. We are friends."

"Hmm." The girl hesitated. "When did I friend you?"

The man looked down at his phone. "In fact, we are more than friends."

Trying to place him among her fairly manageable list of three hundred and twelve friends, Joan said, "I don't think so."

"Listen," the guy said, leaning across the table and whispering in her ear. "I'm the best friend you've got right now. And you better start heeding my messages, or you might end up with the monsters that killed Donna."

Chapter 17

Rico dove into the ocean as if it would hide him forever. The guilt-ridden teen swam deep beneath the surface, holding his breath with furious determination, kicking beyond the breaking waves to escape the detective's words and threats. *I'm innocent*, Rico thought, *but not completely innocent*. Eyes wide, he rose like a pursued fish, bursting into the air and gasping for life.

Rolling on his back, Rico floated beneath a reddening cloud. Yes, he'd met Donna Murskey at a party last December in a mansion on Palm Beach. He'd been paid a hundred dollars to stand in front of the neo-Greek temple because the owner, a man in a scarlet mask, wanted the entrance to resemble the most exclusive nightclub on earth. Gold velvet ropes hung from pillar to pillar, and only "the illumined ones" were allowed to pass through. Rico and some other temps stood on the uninvited side of the velvet ropes.

"Listen up, temps!" Scarlet Mask shouted from the balcony. "I want to see more envy on your faces!"

Red lights flickered through the windows, and there were shouts in the mansion that may have been screams. Rico was repulsed and intrigued by the whole scene.

"More envy! More envy, or I'm not paying you!"

The temps murmured, "Let us in. We want to be let in."

The masked man nodded approvingly, then sneered and disappeared into his temple. Screams of pain and gurgles of red laughter welcomed him back to the murderous lights, and the whole place smelled like flatulence.

A few hours later, with the evening deep into midnight, the man strode outside, grabbed the velvet ropes, and flung them to the ground. "Come on in! Are you eighteen? No matter. You will be of age tonight. Here, we are all old souls. Welcome!"

While the rest of the temps rushed inside, Rico hesitated. He was only seventeen. His parents expected him to be home by ten, and he'd promised to stop by Mia's house for a quick kiss or two. They'd recently started dating, and already they were fairly serious. However, the opportunity to get inside of a Palm Beach mansion was a temptation the kid from the trailer park could not resist. Rico followed the group through the pillars and was astounded by the decorated walls that did not seem Greek (or Roman) but merely gross. The art consisted of long rows of weapons framed by irregular globs of gray and black paint, along with random sprays of red feathers stuck to the walls with what looked like blood. The name of the lunatic claiming to be an artist was an indecipherable scrawl, sickly green, dripping near the mottled marble floor.

A voice screamed, "I'll get you! I'll kill you!"

A skeletal man dressed in a leather diaper ran down the hallway while being chased by a dwarf who was also wearing a diaper. The aggressive dwarf had a whip and snapped at the skeleton. "I'll get you! I'll kill you!"

It was not Halloween, so Rico was a bit freaked out to witness a typical night on Palm Beach. The skeleton disappeared through a secret door of red feathers, leaving the whip-wielding dwarf to toddle up the hallway toward the temp. "I'll get you, Ricardo. I'll kill you."

Rico's initial fear and surprise became military-level bravado. He assumed a semi-kung and fully fu stance, and then spoke with a commanding voice, "Back off, freak! Or I'll take away your whip and, um, whoop you."

"I'll whoop you," the dwarf replied.

"I don't think you will," Rico said. "I'm fairly confident that I'll be doing the whooping here. Okay? Just go back to, um, your dungeon or whatever."

"I'm not going back to the dungeon," the dwarf said, raising the whip. "Not until you're whooped. Understand? No amount of kung or fu can help you now."

Rico wasn't sure if he should fight or just turn around and leave. Not liking either of those options, he chose the middle path between violence and retreat. He took a huge breath and projected what he thought was the sound of a humble eagle. "EEEAHH!" It was more like a proud pterodactyl. And the timing was a little off, because the owner of the mansion appeared and hissed through his mask, "Stop messing with the magic."

"Magic?"

"Yes. The musical, magical flow, the *IS* of the universe."

"What?"

"IS," the mask hissed. "IS, IS, IS!"

Rico had not read the story in the *Palm Beach Post* about how Palm Beach was "the most wicked place on earth," teeming with all sorts of perversion and sorcery. *Who even are you?* Rico thought, staring at the pitiful, powerful billionaire and his diapered dwarf.

At that moment, Donna Murskey came traipsing down the hall, demanding everyone's attention. The girl had a new diamond hanging from a braided silver necklace, and she was dressed like an angel. Not in white, but in blue, shimmering feathers and heavenly shoes with little wings.

"Look at you," Rico said.

She smiled for a moment and took him by the hand. "Let's get out of here. I've had it with these freaks."

Now floating in the ocean, under the watchful eyes of Detective Beauchamp, Rico remembered every detail of that evening. The stroll into the garden, the glittering pond of water colored with koi fish, the candles in the overhanging trees, the scent of gardenia and oleander, and beatific Donna with her shiny diamond. And the kiss. And the guilt.

Chapter 18

Father Pierre splashed in the river, his lungs filling with water and his head losing light while the alligator attacked him. Going numb with pain, the priest made a final effort to rise. He leaned into the current and allowed the powerful flow to lift him while a prayer— *Our Father, who art in Heaven*—kept him from passing out. *Hallowed be thy name* . . . Breaking the surface with a splutter and a cough, he spread his arms for more support . . . *thy Kingdom come* . . . and reached a bloody hand toward shore . . . *thy will be done* . . .

Chapter 19

The bishop sat slumped at his desk, staring at his mother's photograph. "I know, I know," he said. "I must do things correctly. One more mistake could ruin my reputation. If the man from British Petroleum is truly possessed, and if he hurts somebody, I'll be held responsible. This office has failed miserably, almost irreparably, in the past. Things were kept in the darkness that should have been given to the light."

The bishop glanced at a scrap of paper on his desk that had a phone number for a writer at the *Palm Beach Post*.

Looking again at his mother, the bishop said, "I'm going to include Lillian Reynolds on the Spiritual Warfare Committee. I want her to record everything so there will be no questions about transparency. It's time for the church to err on the side of giving out too much information, instead of too little."

"Oh, my sweet James," his mother seemed to say. *"Don't mess this up. Don't make me haunt you."*

Chapter 20

Leaving the coffee shop, Joan and Mia hurried past a horde of reptilian handbags in several window displays and retreated to a more private location. In the middle of Worth Avenue is a "secret garden" open to the public, a geographical oxymoron of great beauty. The girls entered the Via de Lela, a lush hideaway full of green ferns and flowers of every color. Archways of bright, prickly vines guarded the entrance to an inner grotto filled with sculptures of children leap-frogging, swinging, and climbing.

"Listen to what I found out," Mia said.

"I'm listening." Joan stood in direct sunlight near two metallic children. "What did you find out?"

"The jeweler told me that Donna came in early one morning, about a month ago, to have something appraised."

"What a strange life," Joan said. "What teenager wakes up in the morning and has jewelry appraised?"

"Well," Mia said, leaning against a sculpture of a ladder, "it was a diamond."

Horror and intrigue filled Joan's heart. "The killer gave her a gift."

Mia nodded. "A million-dollar gift around her neck."

Gazing at the children frozen in time, Joan asked, "Does the jeweler know who gave the diamond to Donna?"

"No. The sale was handled by a fake security company."

"Hmm, I suppose we should tell the cops."

"The cops already know," Mia said. "Detective Beauchamp interviewed the jeweler yesterday."

"Wow, it seems like you got the jeweler to tell you everything."

Mia laughed. "Well, I plied him."

"You *what*?"

"I plied him with a venti caramel double-dolphin dare vanilla latte Fountain of Youth. With four shots. And his tongue flowed with information. Also, he seemed distraught and needed to vent. You know I'm an excellent listener."

Joan looked away, as if not wanting to know more. "What else did he say?"

"He said it was known on Worth Avenue that Donna was involved with the WINGS."

"Wealth Initiative . . . something."

"Networking Group for Society. Remember? A group of rich old men. The jeweler said the WINGS own the world and give small amounts of money to charity to get their pictures in the news. So they appear to be angels of society. But they're also the sponsors of the Demon Dance."

"The WINGS are not angelic," Joan said, her eyes flashing. "And if they sponsor demonic activity, they're begging to be doomed."

"Preach it, girl."

"I'm no preacher, but a Demon Dance? Really?"

"Yeah, I know. So tell me what the guy in the corner said to you, the guy with the gorgeous head of hair. Not that we're focused on that. But it was amazing hair. Just saying."

Pausing to answer, Joan climbed a metal swing and tugged on the sculpted ropes, trying to move the immovable object.

Mia raised her voice. "Tell me what the guy with the hair said. He seemed to have some good information."

"He said," Joan whispered, still trying to force the swing to break free from its welding, "the WINGS and I will fight. And it will be to the death."

Chapter 21

Mother Heron's garden was a paradise of fruits and flowers, including scarlet sage clustered in foot-high flames near the cabin. On the door was a large work of beaded art, an image of the Virgin Mary reclining beneath a many-colored tree. When Mother Heron wasn't working in her garden, she sat on the porch, contemplating the great play of light and shadow in the wilderness.

"Help," she heard someone gasp.

Mother Heron stood. "Who needs help? Where are you? I don't see you."

"Help," she heard again. The sound was weaker.

Immediately the old woman scrambled down the steps to the shoreline, and began searching for the source of the cry. Several times in the past, she'd been able to save people from drowning in the murky river. Now, not seeing or hearing anyone, she hurried along a narrow, precarious path and looked around the bend. *Lots of hidden branches here*, she thought. *This is where most things get caught*. Mother Heron leaned over the edge of the river, careful to keep her balance. "Oh," she whispered. "Oh no."

There was blood in the water.

And two alligators circling a body.

Chapter 22

Retreating to his garden behind the cathedral, the bishop sat on a bench in the shade. He wished he could simply relax and enjoy a good book, perhaps escape in some idyllic, placid pastoral, but truly, his work in the tempestuous world was never done. "Looks like rain," he muttered, and then took out his phone to call a young reporter at the newspaper.

"Lillian, hello."

"Hey there, Bish," she said, standing on the sidewalk outside of her building. She took a drag on her cigarette. "Are you calling to receive information, or to give information?"

"I'm calling to talk about the weather," he said dryly. "Have you ever seen such extremes of fair and foul?"

Lil quipped, "Are you talking about the weather or my love life?"

The bishop paused, realizing he shouldn't waste time with worldly banter. "I need your help," he said, voice lowering to a whisper. "The Murskey girl. What really happened to her?"

Lil took a deep drag on her cigarette and blew the smoke into the phone. "I don't know more than I've already told you. Give me another day or two."

"Okay, Lillian, good. But another reason I'm calling is to ask you about joining something."

She sucked more smoke and chuckled. "You want me to play on your softball team? Hoping to beat the Mormons this year?"

A bird screeched a sort of song from behind the statue of the Virgin, followed by another screech further into the garden. "I'm serious, Lillian."

"What? I can't hear you."

The screech-singing birds were joined by a gray helicopter buzzing over the cathedral. The helicopter circled twice around the building, making a whirlwind of leaves and debris, and then hightailed toward the Everglades.

"Bish? You still there?"

"I'm still here, Lillian," he said, watching the copter shrink to the size of a dragonfly. "I have a favor to ask."

"Okay. Ask away."

"You recall our last conversation."

"Yes."

"We agreed that the cathedral and the media should be friends, not enemies."

"Yes."

"Lillian, I'm going to ask you to do something extremely important. I expect you'll say no, because it could be a no-win situation."

"Sounds like quite a challenge. What is it?"

The bishop paused, knowing his words would strike her as very odd. "Lillian, I'm asking you to be a member of a church committee."

She shrieked with laughter. "You're out of your mind!"

"Pardon?"

"Um, sorry, Bish. It's not you, it's me. I'm just not the type to sit around a table with knitting needles, talking about bake sales."

"It's the Spiritual Warfare Committee."

"Spiritual Warfare Committee," the reporter said, blowing smoke toward the sky. "That's some assignment."

"It's not an assignment. It's a friendly request. I want you to record everything that happens. And it might include an exorcism."

"For real?"

"Lillian, your job will be to render the truth, the whole truth, of souls caught up in a cosmic battle."

"Holy crap."

"Is that a yes or a no?"

The reporter laughed and spat her cigarette on the wet sidewalk, where it sizzled and hissed. "Yes."

Chapter 23

"Al-la-pat-tah!" Mother Heron shouted at the nearest alligator. *"Hampi!"*

The reptile had tasted human flesh and wanted a bigger chunk, but the old woman's words made the blood-toothed beast turn and slither downstream.

"Al-la-pat-tah!" Mother yelled at the second alligator. "Git!"

The fifteen-foot monster lurched as if speared and splashed away, leaving a bloody Father Pierre bobbing just above the surface, caught on some branches. The Seminole woman had seen her share of corpses in the river. She recalled a drunken old fisherman who fell overboard, and she could picture the teenage boy who dared to swim in the Loxahatchee at dusk, feeding time for the gators. And there was a murder victim a few years back, a businessman from New Orleans, an unsolved case.

Mother Heron struggled to pull the Haitian to shore, dragging him through the mud into a cluster of dry grass where she fell, exhausted, but did not drop the man. Holding the priest in her arms, she said a silent prayer. The man's skin was cold when she kissed the gentle face that, even in death, seemed full of love and mercy. *I'm so sorry I couldn't save you. I'm so sorry.*

And there, in the mud and the blood and the weeds, surrounded by all the creatures of the wilderness, the man opened his eyes and gasped for air.

Chapter 24

Rico, wreathed in seaweed, floated further out into the ocean, his eyes squinting at the sky while his face was salted by tears and lapping waves.

"I didn't kill Donna," he said to the sunlight. "I tried to help her."

Detective Beauchamp shouted from the shore, "Ricardo, swim back here! Now!" Beauchamp's face was as red as the lifeguard's who whistled to alert the beachgoers that a shark had been spotted. In fact, the water was full of shadows.

In his own world, Rico had no awareness of the sharks between him and the beach. Further and further out, he floated to the edge of the Gulf Stream, lost in memories and daydreams of his second love.

He closed his eyes. "I only kissed her. I never hurt her."

The shadows continued to hunt the mournful young man.

"Ricardo!" Beauchamp raised a bullhorn and tried to summon him, worried that the sharks might silence his "person of interest." The floater heard nothing but the memory of Donna in his ears, and it sounded like a rhythmic weeping.

Donna had opened her soul to Rico one night in her room, telling him how she'd fallen in with the WINGS. "They know how far the flesh can go," she said, standing near an open window. The girl watched a harvest moon slowly rise out of the ocean. "There's nothing left, nothing real or imaginary. I can't really explain it. It's just that I've been everywhere with these people, around and around. And the only place left is the tomb."

Closing the curtains, Donna faced the boy who was intently listening. "It's gone too far," she said, wiping a tear. "Rico, it's gone all the way back to the beginning. Not the good beginning of love in the Garden. No, it's returned to the bad beginning, with the Liar and the Dragon. The WINGS want to make everyone fall again."

The fear in her voice compelled the boy to embrace her. Rico held Donna near the edge of the bed, held her more passionately than a friend should, despite what he had with Mia and despite how the last thing Donna needed was a lover. In fact, considering the danger she was in, what the girl really needed was a bodyguard.

Innocent, guilty, innocent, guilty . . .

The ocean current carried Rico beyond where anyone would venture in a little wooden rowboat, so the panicked lifeguard phoned for the Coast Guard, shouting, "We need a helicopter!"

Spinner sharks circled all around Rico while he blindly floated toward the Virgin Islands, whispering, "I should have protected her. I should have tried harder to save her."

Chapter 25

Father Adam sat uncomfortably in a dented, youth-group canoe on the Loxahatchee River. He hadn't canoed in forty years, or perhaps fifty, so he wobbled and nearly capsized under a scaly palm tree that resembled a dinosaur neck. "Whoa, Nessie," he said, smacking at the water instead of paddling. His purple shirt was blotched by splashes of rust-colored river water, but at least his pants were still dry. He took that as a good sign and kept on going, almost toppling around every bend.

Eventually gaining control in a straightaway, the retired exorcist lit a cigarette, coughed and gasped, and blew a cloud of smoke that joined the afternoon haze of the jungle. "This place is like a psalm," he whispered. "This place is mourning something."

Somewhere among the trees, a wild peacock cried out.

Father Adam sighed and drifted away from the loudly lamenting bird. "What am I doing out here?" An hour ago, he'd been sitting in his cozy cottage, feeling relatively strong while battling the twerkers on TV. Now the Loxahatchee filled the old exorcist with a sense of impending death. He could feel and envision a gloom of centuries floating through the Kingdom of Florida, from the saber-toothed tigers and mastodons of the early forest, to the ghostly dream of Ponce de Leon hunting the wrong grail, to the Seminoles fighting to keep the river free from the confluence of trails and tears.

"What am I doing out here?"

He steered a middle course through the wilderness, sometimes hurrying as if to minister at an emergency, and sometimes drifting as if there was nothing on earth to do but witness whatever presented itself. "Well, I'll be." A blue heron stood in half-shade, one foot on shore and the other in the water, snake-necked and poised to strike. While the old priest glided near, ripples broke the surface, revealing glints of swarming fish. The bird did not blink while attacking the alluring lights, the lethal beak plunging like a dagger to pierce the wriggling flesh.

53

The peacock cried up the river, more melodic at a distance, an echoing song.

"I remember this place," the exorcist said dreamily. "I always loved this lost world. Yes, I do love it."

In the reflection of trees and sky, he floated while the last rays of light fizzled through the forest. The exorcist had seen the worst shadows in the world—the scorched fallen spirits—and so the dusky wilderness wasn't very frightening to him, nor was the water moccasin staring from the shore, or the alligator eyes in the middle of the river.

"Make way," Father Adam said. "Be gone!"

The alligator remained in the center of the current, unblinking, unmoving, as if guarding some flesh or other treasure beneath the surface.

"Make way!"

The canoe was on a collision course with the monster, and the old priest refused to veer around or placate the beast in any way.

"By God, be gone!"

The blood-toothed gator bit the canoe as if to get a small taste, and then submerged, disappearing into the murk.

Father Adam knew never to look back at what he'd rebuked. When a spiritual pest was disempowered, it was best to ignore it and show neither fear nor pride.

Hissing, the monster resurfaced like a long dark spirit behind the canoe. The beast seemed to be hunting the exorcist as if to avenge an old wound.

Chapter 26

Dear Reader, if being pursued by snakes and alligators is not your cup of double-dolphin dare, then I must give you another warning: this story will only get worse. Yes, Florida is the perfect place for all of your favorite, hideous beasts.

And there will be a dragon.

Chapter 27

Joan and Mia were having lunch at Shipwreck Deli on Palm Beach, eating smoked salmon on bagels and eavesdropping on conversations. It seemed like everyone was talking about Donna's murder and what it meant in the grand scheme of things. "It's the end of the world," an old woman said, munching on turkey pastrami. "The rye bread is fresh today, unlike yesterday, but I'm telling you—it's the end of the world."

Joan shook her head, and also nodded agreement, while Mia glanced at her phone. "Unknown number, but the text is from Rico. He says he's in the hospital!"

Not wanting more drama, Joan said, "He's just playing a trick. You know how he is, always messing with you."

"No. Rico's really in the hospital! He's at Good Samaritan."

"Relax. I'm sure it's only a joke."

"How can you be sure? Rico doesn't joke about important things, just stupid things. This is important, right? We're talking about the freaking hospital!"

"Don't freak," Joan said. "Just call the number back. And I'll dial Rico. We'll know the truth in a minute."

"Okay."

A minute later, despite putting so much faith in phones, there was no response.

"Let's go!" Mia said, standing and waving her arms. "It's real. Rico's really hurt! I can feel his pain!"

"Okay, okay, let's go to the hospital."

The girls slapped some cash on the table and rushed out to the parking lot.

"Let me drive," Mia said.

"No," Joan answered.

"I'm an awesome driver," Mia said. "I can get to the hospital faster than you can."

"No way. Nobody drives my truck except for me."

"This isn't the time to be so possessive, but whatever. Let's go!"

They jumped in the old rustbucket and Joan accelerated out of the lot, around the corner, and toward the bridge while Mia reached over and blared the horn. "Get going, you idiots! What a bunch of idiots! Especially you, Rolls Royce!"

"You're making things worse," Joan said. "Just try to be calm."

Taking a break from honking, Mia dialed Rico's number. "Pick up! Pick up!" Then she dialed the unknown number. "Pick up! Pick up!" But nobody answered.

"Drive faster!" Mia said. "Hurry, before the bridge goes up and traps us on Palm Beach!"

The alarm sounded, the warning light flashed red, and the long arm of the bridge came down. Adrenaline flowing, Joan swerved around a black hearse and floored the accelerator, intent on smashing through the safety arm and making the leap.

"Yes, you can do it," Mia said. "You can fly across that bridge."

It was unlikely, but possible. Other people in history were known to have flown, or at least floated on the air for a while, falling from great heights without quite dying. However, common sense inspired our heroine to hit the brakes. The old truck skidded to a stop just behind the safety arm, and Joan put it in park.

Mia yelled, "Keep going! What if Rico dies and I'm not there to say goodbye?"

"You'll see him soon enough. Just try to relax." Joan spoke as calmly as possible while the center of the bridge began to rise and make a chasm. "I'm sure Rico is fine. He probably twisted an ankle or something."

Mia Kittinger, the valedictorian who had spoken at graduation about the importance of good decisions, unbuckled her seatbelt, scooted over, and stomped her foot on the accelerator. "I love him,

Joan! I love him!" The engine roared and roared, but the Chevy didn't move. Because it was in park.

"Mia, don't mess with the engine. What are you doing? Chill!"

Visualizing Rico gasping for breath in the hospital, Mia reached out and shifted the truck into drive. It was a very mystical moment, partly because of Mia's insane love for Rico, and mostly because everyone in the world who has gotten stopped by a drawbridge has felt the heroic impulse to smash through the safety arm and go flying across the Chasm of Doom. Mia shouted manically, "Here we go!" The Chevy squealed its tires and raced forward, busting the safety arm and rocketing up the incline of the lifting bridge.

Fighting Mia for control of the truck, Joan shouted, "We can't jump the gap! What are you doing? We'll crash into the water and drown!"

The bridge monitor in the tower, affectionately known as The Troll, was somewhat surprised to see a vehicle break through the barrier, yet he tried to maintain a proper trollish professionalism, recalling the five minutes of intensive training he'd received regarding this type of situation. He grabbed for the emergency phone and knocked it on the floor. "Crap." Then he lurched around, searching for the switch to stop the bridge from lifting—too late—so he just sat in his chair and watched the Chevy launch like a daredevil machine, sparks flying as if to signal a fiery catastrophe.

Chapter 28

Dear Reader, don't blame me. I didn't teach Mia how to drive. And I didn't give The Troll his five minutes of emergency training.

Chapter 29

At the Havana Restaurant walk-up window, the reporter held her phone under her chin and reached for a cup of *café con leche*. Lil took a sip of the frothy nectar, licked away the sugary moustache, and proceeded with the conversation. "There's a wide chasm between us, Bish, but I accept your offer to be on the Spiritual Warfare Committee. Be forewarned, however, that I'll disclose everything, the whole truth, and nothing but the truth."

"Okay," the bishop said, using the old landline phone at his desk. "Okay. Excellent."

Lil walked around the Havana building toward the parking lot while the clouds rumbled and flashed a little light. "I'll be a good committee member, Bish, but you need to understand that I won't be part of any cover-up. I'm going to record and report everything that happens, even if fire shoots from your nostrils."

"Fire from my nostrils?" the bishop asked, confused.

"Yes. If that happens, I'll have to report it."

"What?"

"I'm just kidding."

The bishop paused, wiped his brow, and laughed. "I remember your Confirmation, Lillian, and I believe you giggled through the whole thing."

"It wasn't my fault. One of the altar boys couldn't stop farting. It wasn't incense, and it wasn't exactly inspiring."

"Well, we make our rituals as reverent as possible, given the problematic nature of our earthiness."

Lil opened the door of her Subaru. "As reverent as possible? Apparently, you haven't been reading Fr. Z's blog. There was a post yesterday about a yodeling cowboy priest who floated into church on a hover board."

"Ugh." The bishop chose his other words very carefully. "Indeed, we have some serious issues to address regarding rubrics and how they affect praxis."

From high above the cathedral, a gray helicopter whooshed down and began circling, creating a whirlwind of dust and debris that battered against the bishop's office window. "Oh, not again. Why do they keep bugging us?"

Lil heard the commotion while she climbed into her white Outback. Careful not to spill her coffee, she put the key in the ignition and leaned forward to allow the air conditioning to blast her face. It felt like a cool ocean breeze in a furnace, but a high-pitched squealing accompanied the flow of cold air, making the car sound a bit possessed.

"Sorry about that, Lillian," the bishop said, almost hollering into the phone. "A helicopter keeps bugging the church for some reason. Maybe you could investigate that."

The reporter took another gulp of coffee. The creamy elixir filled her with a pleasant tingling, and yet there was a pain in her heart.

"Confession time," Lil said, wiping her mouth.

Not sure if she was being serious, the bishop responded, "Really? What do you have to confess, Lillian?"

She sped toward the newspaper building, swerving around a migrant mother who was pushing a wobbly stroller across the street. "I suppose you've heard every sort of confession under the sun."

"Yes, Lillian. There is nothing you can say that I haven't heard before."

Lil guzzled the last of the *café con leche*. "What if God refuses to hear? Maybe that's why he drowned out the world one time. He didn't want to listen anymore."

"I don't follow. What are you saying?"

The gray helicopter kept circling around the cathedral and shining lights upon the ground as if hunting for something. The bishop literally had to yell, "Tell me what's on your heart, Lillian!"

Speeding through a red light, the reporter whispered, "I hurt . . . I hurt . . ."

And the bishop's phone went dead.

Chapter 30

Joan and Mia floated in the air between the gaping jaws of the bridge. They were about to crash and burn, or crash and drown, or crash and survive for a few minutes before being devoured by sharks or giant eels or whatever hideous creatures roamed the waterway into which the old Chevy would plunge and burst into oily flames.

"Yes! It's working!" Mia continued to lean over and press her foot on the accelerator. "We're almost across! We're flying, Joan! We're flying!"

The Chevy roared across the chasm, wheels whirring and lightning flashing as if signaling a major cosmic event, and the truck kept flying like a rusty miracle and not an earthly contraption that seemed doomed to fall, until, eventually, it began to fall.

"I was right," Joan whispered. "We're going to die."

Yes, Joan was right. They were going to die. Just like all of us.

But not yet.

With a fluttering noise that almost sounded like wings, the Chevy soared to the other side of the bridge—landing with a loud scraping bounce and making a great cloud of flickering sparks shooting like stars.

"Woo-hoo!" Mia shouted.

"Wow," Joan said, surprised. "We didn't die. We actually flew."

The Chevy crashed through another barrier and careened to the right, barely making the turn on Flagler Drive without hitting the historic fishing shack or the geezer with a dapper hat who just wanted to go for a stroll along the waterway before the storm arrived. "Dern flying kids!" he shouted, shaking his fist.

Joan gave Mia a shove. "Put your seatbelt on and stay seated. We're in big trouble."

Sirens blared from both sides of the bridge because The Troll had stepped on the emergency phone and then randomly dialed several numbers on his own phone, including 911, and reported: "Two females just jumped the bridge. What? Yes, they did. No, not with motorcycles. They're driving a Chevy truck that I suspect was stolen. And one of the females has heliotrope hair, so I'm sure they're armed and dangerous."

Joan accelerated toward the hospital while Mia checked her phone to see if she'd missed a text from Rico when they were airborne. "Nothing," she said. "Hurry, Joan, hurry!"

Racing along the waterway, Joan gripped the wheel with trembling fingers and remembered the rainy morning when her father was leaving for the Middle East, and how he'd ceremoniously given her the keys to the pickup. "This is an early birthday present, kiddo. Treat the old Chevy good, okay? Drive slow and safe, keep her full of oil, and you'll always get wherever you need to go."

In the rearview mirror and through the windows, Joan saw lightning and the lights of law enforcement.

"Sorry, Dad," she whispered, and accelerated to a more dangerous speed.

The glow of sky, city, and water all blurred like an impressionistic painting, as if the heavens and earth were just dreamy works of art, and then the sign for Good Samaritan Hospital appeared in perfect clarity.

Joan yanked the wheel to the left and sped toward the main entrance while Mia opened her door as if to leap into the large red plants rising like flames of passion near the valet parking area. Joan hit the brakes and Mia immediately jumped out and dashed frantically up the stairs. "Rico!" she said, with enough melodrama to make everyone in the hospital sick. "Hold on, Rico! Don't die before I say I love you!"

Chapter 31

The old exorcist, floating down the Loxahatchee River, was a bit spooked by the thunder, and by the reptilian eyes glowing at the surface. Father Adam's hands were starting to shake and his stomach was rumbling, and he seriously questioned why he'd been inspired to embark on this quest. The river had taken him deep into the wilderness, and he would not be able to paddle out during the night. So he was trapped by momentum, whether spiritual or earthly, with no other option than to continue forward. A canoe topples easily, and one wrong move would make a meal for alligators.

The priest squinted at a blurry shoreline, knowing the land was as dangerous as the water, with mama gators nesting among weeds, ready to kill anything that trespassed near their eggs. Father Adam maneuvered the canoe as best he could, through spider-webbed branches and around cypress logs that floated like dead bodies.

I'm dead, he thought, surrounded by more and more eyes. *I'll never survive the night.*

That thought was immediately followed by a howl and a shriek.

What on earth?

During the many exorcisms he'd performed, Father Adam had heard every sort of cry that a human or devil can make. The howl and the shriek on the river were different. Wilder. More powerful. Filling the wilderness with a tangible energy.

The canoe nearly collided with a pair of glowing eyes, and the lights submerged into nothingness while a quickening current dragged the exorcist around a bend. In a flash of lightning, cypress trees grew into sky-monsters, their branches like tentacles reaching down for prey. "I'm dead," he whispered, and then he wished, knowing it was not the most reverent desire, for a final smoke.

At that moment, a tiny flame appeared beyond the shoreline, a sun-colored shimmer. The light danced around trees and through ferns, making a thousand green halos and showing a narrow golden path from the cabin to the riverside. Voices like crazed laughter, like the allure of mirth mixed with mischief, enticed the priest to paddle toward shore to investigate this new mystery. In his haste, he accidentally slapped the head of an alligator and the beast immediately arose from the water and snapped at his arm—barely missing—before splashing back down to the river. The exorcist paddled furiously forward, hitting another gator while the current tried to pull the canoe away. "No you don't. No you don't." Father Adam plunged his paddle down into the mud and forced the canoe on shore.

Slithering behind him were more than a dozen gators, swarming as if they smelled blood in the water. In fact, a few hours earlier the blood of Father Pierre had flowed over that very spot, riling up the monsters and energizing them to seek more human flesh.

The exorcist stepped out of the canoe, careful not to slip in the mud, not looking behind at several killers converging upon him. The sky growled loudly while huge raindrops fell, drawing the man's eyes heavenward. Jaws opened and fiery teeth approached his flesh for a simple, instinctive kill. The priest would have been rolled to the river's depths and devoured, except a voice shrieked through the rain, the words impossible to decipher. The monsters were startled by the voice and retreated into the water, their glowing eyes going dark. In a sizzle of lightning, an old woman appeared at the shoreline. Her face was like cypress bark, and she extended a bony hand. "Welcome," she called through the storm. "Welcome to this side of Eden."

Father Adam clutched his canoe paddle with one hand and reached with the other to shake the cold flesh. "Who are you?" he asked.

With a giggle, the old woman tried to pull him toward higher ground while he slipped on the slope and muttered, "Don't kill me. Whoever you are, you don't have to kill me. I'm barely alive the way it is."

She released him and pointed—her arm like another branch of lightning—to the cabin suffused with candlelight. "I know why you were sent," she said. "I know why you were summoned. Do you know why?"

Father Adam gritted his teeth and tried to discern the source of such powerful energy emanating from the strange woman. During his exorcisms, he'd felt the presence of evil as a chill, or an odor, or an electricity that raised the hair on his neck. The old woman was both cold and fiery, smelled of soil and sky, and seemed charged with an otherworldly power.

"I have your friend," she said, grinning, raindrops rolling down her face. "I retrieved the body from the bloody water."

The priest leaned closer and tried to discern the spirit of her words. Demons were ever-lying, and if this woman spoke with a serpent's tongue, then he'd know her energy was negative. He took a deep breath and made the sign of the Cross. *"Domine sancte, Pater omnipotens,"* he intoned, watching for her reaction.

The rain fell darker, swirling around in a bedraggling wind. The woman's hair was like a mess of snakes, hissing in the storm. She cackled, "I have him! I have the other priest! I have what the alligators left for me!"

Shivering from the rain and the unknown, Father Adam felt weary and powerless. He'd never encountered anything like this. The old woman spoke with a frightening authority.

"You will go to my cabin," she said, grabbing his trembling hand. "You will see what remains of your friend."

Chapter 32

"They tried to devour me," Rico said, dramatizing his oceanic ordeal for an elderly lady at the welcome desk of the hospital. He limped to and fro, almost knocking over a stack of insurance brochures while gesticulating wildly. "The devilish sharks turned the water into a cauldron! Bubbling, twisting waves! The spinners flew all around me, their jaws chomping!"

"I know the feeling," the lady said. "I have twelve grandchildren."

Rico had drained three cups of coffee in the hospital. "And then a giant bird descended from the heavens and swooped upon the ocean to save me!"

The welcome lady shook her head and scoffed. "A giant bird? That was a helicopter."

Rico's hand shot skyward. "And a glorious ladder, dazzling like diamonds, was lowered from the belly of the heavenly bird!"

"It was a Coast Guard helicopter."

"Huh? No, it was a mystical bird."

The old woman tried not to smirk. "We pay taxes so the Coast Guard can save people like you."

"People like me? You know what? I'm becoming an Army Ranger."

"Oh, dear," the volunteer said.

"Rico! Rico!"

Mia rushed through the door. "You're alive!" She saw a large bandage wrapped around her boyfriend's leg. "What happened?"

He grinned. "Killer sharks tried to kill me."

Mia felt faint. "You were attacked by sharks?"

The welcome lady shook her head and scoffed. "They were little spinners. The boy was merely grazed, not bitten. He's already been released."

"Oh, Rico! You're alive and well!"

"And talking," the lady said with a sigh. She looked down at a magazine, allowing the teens to enjoy their drama.

Rico opened his arms for a hug. "C'mere, Freckles."

Mia embraced him as if he were the greatest thing on earth, her tears drenching both of their faces. Rico blushed, ashamed by how much she loved him. Did he love her nearly as much? Some words tried to work their way to Rico's lips, a confession about Donna Murskey. However, instead of confessing, he gave Mia a passionate, guilty kiss.

Chapter 33

Lil stared at a blank computer screen in her cubicle in the newspaper building. Her fingers were poised at the keyboard, ready to start clacking away while her brain flared with endorphins from the *café con leche*. The story "The Exorcism of Superstition" was ready to be written and the message would be simple: exorcism was outdated and should be outlawed.

Lil's phone rang, and she hesitated before answering. "Hey, Bish."

"What did you want to confess?"

"Confess? What are you talking about?"

"Before we were cut off, Lillian, you wanted to confess something."

A wave of thunder hit the newspaper building, shaking her desk. "I did?"

"Yes. Unless I misunderstood your words."

The reporter began typing: *I agreed to be part of an exorcism team. Appointed by the Bishop of the Palm Beach Diocese, I was assigned the role of truth teller. Perhaps in another age, I would have been called The Soothsayer.*

"Lillian? Did I misunderstand your words?"

Lightning flashed and Lil held her fingers above the keyboard as if levitating on electricity. "Bish, I need to clarify something—before you get too deep into this."

"Yes. I'm listening."

Lil's computer screen flickered. Her words glowed red and disappeared. "Dang. That's an interesting coincidence."

"Excuse me, Lillian?"

"Excuse you for what? Did you burp?"

There was an awkward pause, punctuated by Lil's nervous laughter. "I'm sorry, Bish. Please forgive me. My nerves are fried. I haven't been sleeping well, and the amount of caffeine in my bloodstream could power a nuclear submarine."

"I understand."

She sighed and was actually frustrated with the bishop for being so understanding. She almost wished he'd take on a persona of pomposity and threaten her with fire and brimstone. "Listen," she told him, "you need to understand something. My instinct is to write a very negative story about this whole business."

"I understand."

Pointing her index finger, Lil reached out and touched the computer screen, and received a powerful shock. "Ouch! Listen, Bish, you know I can't write nonsense about the so-called spiritual world. I'm going to clarify this story for the reader. And right now, I think the story is this: exorcism is fake."

The bishop stared at a painting of Saint Michael stomping on Satan while lightning flashed through his office window and made the devil's eyes glow. "Lillian, I trust you as a journalist. I've read many of your stories. Even when you're tough on members of the clergy, you're fair. And you know what? That's all I can ask, considering all of our sins. Just hate us fairly. And love us fairly, too."

Lil's fingers sizzled on the keyboard. "I'm quoting you about that hate and love thing."

"That's fine. Everything I say is on the record."

"Excellent. Now we're talking. So tell me, who are the other members of the Spiritual Warfare Committee?"

"Well, the confirmed members would be me, you, Mrs. Teffler, and Father Pierre. We're also trying to recruit Father Cranky Pants, I mean Father Adam, and a holy woman who lives on the river."

Lil tried not to giggle. "Cranky Pants?"

"Please don't call him Cranky Pants."

"I thought you weren't going to tell me what to write."

"I won't. But please don't write Cranky Pants."

"No promises, Bish. Now seriously, do you actually know a holy woman? That sounds so mythical. A holy woman—in this millennium?"

"Yes," the bishop said without hesitation. "I've met about five people in my life that were, well, sort of superhuman."

"Five? That sounds like a lot."

"Considering that I've met thousands of people in my life, five is not exactly a large percentage."

"But even one holy person, in this day and age. I don't think anyone would believe it, unless you have solid evidence."

"Her name is Mother Heron."

"Mother . . . Heron? Oh, I think I remember reading about her. She was famous back in the day for her political activism. She must be ancient by now."

"Yes, I sent Father Pierre to her cabin to explain the situation and invite her to town. But I haven't received an update. I'm starting to get worried."

"And what about Cranky Pants? I mean, Father Adam? Didn't he retire under a cloud of scandal? Weren't there mistresses involved?"

The bishop turned his gaze to the photo of his mother. "No. Father Adam retired in the good graces of the Church. There was one woman involved, but the relationship was pure."

Lil laughed. "A pure relationship between a man and a woman. Yeah, right."

"I'm telling you the truth."

"If you say so. Then let me ask you another question, for the sake of truth."

"Okay. Ask away."

"Have any of your holy or unholy priests heard a confession of murder recently?"

The bishop paused. "I cannot answer that."

"You cannot answer? Really? For the sake of transparency, aren't you going to reveal the truth? Tell me, Bish. Do you already know who killed Donna Murskey?"

Another pause, and more lightning. Florida seemed to be all thunder and fire. Every building was shaking.

"Tell me. Was it one of your priests that killed her?"

Chapter 34

The Haitian scholar lay sprawled on a palm-frond cot, his leg bandaged where a gator had bitten him. "Look how I survived the death," Father Pierre said. "Mother Heron is the healer. She made me laugh, and she cleaned the wound, and the pain was horrible. And now I'm the smiling one."

The old exorcist stared at his fellow priest and said nothing.

"Gators have filthy mouths," Mother Heron said. "So I sanitized Father Pierre's wound with bleach, stitched him up, and fed him a good dinner of antibiotics."

Father Pierre sat up on the cot and gestured toward the shelves stacked high with items lost by inexperienced kayakers, canoeists, and boaters. "The river gives her many blessings. Mother would be the wealthy one in my village. She would be the royal one."

"So much stuff," Father Adam said, astounded by the many bags of chips and cookies, plastic plates, hats, caps, visors, umbrellas, fishing rods, reels, tackle boxes, beer coolers, and first-aid kits. He noticed a large pile of cigarette packs and saw his brand, Lucky Strike. "Oh, Mother Heron, may I have a smoke?"

"If that lightning keeps striking," she said, "we'll all be smoking."

Father Pierre howled with laughter, and the old woman stood over his cot and shrieked. They'd been making each other laugh for several hours, ever since she'd pulled a needle through his flesh.

"Have a Lucky Strike," she told the exorcist, her words followed by thunder and a sizzle.

"Thank you." The exorcist fished out a cigarette from one of the packs. "I hate to expedite my demise, but then again, I'm old enough to know I can't defeat death."

"Of course you can defeat death," Mother Heron said. "That's the point of living."

"Mother is one for the warfare," Father Pierre said. He gazed admiringly at her ancient face. "I told her about the man who is possessed, and how we must help him by fighting what is inside of him."

Father Adam scoffed under his breath and lit the Lucky Strike. "Don't try to recruit me. We're done talking about that. I'm finished with that business." He went to the door of the cabin and opened it to exhale a cloud of smoke, hoping the wind wouldn't let in the rain, and at that very moment the storm halted. The night became calm and silent, except for a slow dripping from the cypress trees, the drips like heavy tears, reminding the old priest of so many funerals. It seemed like he'd suffered through a thousand of them, doing his best to alleviate the suffering of others. And then he remembered another sort of crying, the ecstatic tears of a person delivered, how the service of grace would work with just a few words, the loveliest and most powerful words, dripping on a soul and washing it clean.

Oh, what the heck, Father Adam thought, taking another drag of his cigarette. *I guess I can serve on a final committee before I croak.*

Chapter 35

In the center of Palm Beach, a cobra statue was striking in the moonlight, fangs glistening, guarding the path to a midnight garden. The serpent's eyes blazed and its lower body was coiled and recoiling around itself as if the serpent had risen not from the earth but from its own writhing netherworld.

A man masked in shadow, known to a select few as the Ninth One, stood behind the idol, waiting for his prey and pondering the rest of humanity. *All fools,* he thought. *All fools, with a few useful idiots.*

Something squeezed between the iron bars of the gate. It was the man from British Petroleum. "We have been summoned," he said. He placed his fedora upon the head of the cobra. "Hello to all of us. Is it midnight?"

"It is almost midnight," the Ninth One answered. He did not show himself, but continued to speak from behind the serpent. "It may be a strike away. Now speak about the trouble. Whisper into the cobra's ear."

A coil of lightning writhed through the sky, threatening rain or something worse.

"There is hell within the well beneath the Everglades," the Brit whispered. "It seems to go all the way down."

"All the way down," the Ninth One echoed. "We knew that was a possibility. We were warned by engineers of both the light and the dark. And they also warned of methane. But let us not speak of that here. Let us go deeper."

"Oh yes, let us go then, you and us, when the garden is laid out like a corpse upon a funeral pyre."

"You first," the cobra seemed to say.

The Brit leered down the garden path. "I see glimpses of the nymphs. You know how much I love little nymphs. I believe that is how you and us became friends—in the grove of the Bohemian pleasures. May we see them face to face?"

"Face to face?" In a scarlet mask, the Ninth One appeared from behind the serpent.

"Ha!" the Brit said. "Faces to faces!" He put on his hat and rubbed a dark smudge on his gray suit. "May we have the pleasure?"

"Yes."

Past eerie eyes and rising steam, the two men walked further into the garden, winding along a pathway sided by bronze statues of shrieking beasts and carved hedges in the shape of half-human, half-animal chimeras, into another realm of the WINGS. "We paid dearly for this," the Ninth One said. "You need to know we paid dearly for all of this."

"Oh, here they are," the Brit said, giggling.

"Blessed little nymphs. And look, they're not even running away. They must know we're here to adore them."

Statues of adolescent girls, perfectly smooth and firm, were posed near benches where creepers could sit and stare at them without being arrested. One of the girls was named *Youth*, her body stretched skyward, clothed by nothing except the sultry air.

"My love," the Ninth One said, sliding his hands across her torso.

The Brit leaned close to the other girl, *Innocence*. "Did you miss us?" he hissed. "Well, now we shall dance!" He grabbed the small hand of the statue as if expecting *Innocence* to spring into action.

"Listen," the Ninth One said, still groping *Youth*. "We need to speak with that young reporter. We need her to write about our charitable works. Not the other works."

With a murderous look in his eyes, the Brit tugged the hand of *Innocence*. "Should the reporter be spoken to, or touched?"

"That depends. How much does she know?"

"Not everything. Unless she found out today."

Lightning fell near the men, and smoke swirled around them, filling the garden with a hundred more snakes.

The Ninth One frowned. "Will you be in charge of the touching?"

Rubbing his face on the arm of *Innocence*, the Brit answered, "I cannot touch the reporter myself, but Lillian Reynolds will be touched. However, be warned, she knows many cops, including Beauchamp."

Up from the ground arose a flash of lightning—striking at the clouds as if ripping open a wound of rain. The Ninth One cast a confident eye above the royal palms. "Beauchamp is nothing to us. He has no power of discernment. He believes that a local boy touched Donna. And we will keep him thinking that."

The Brit stopped fondling *Innocence* and turned his attention to *Youth*. "They think what we want them to think. Are you making progress with the witch?"

"Joan will soon be ours," the Ninth One said. "Her power is her vulnerability, and she will become an asset for us." He reached over and tapped the BP executive above his heart. "Tell me more about the Florida underworld. Is it true that we've gone all the way down? Is the methane monster really coming up?"

"Oh, we have the monster under control," he lied. "I don't think there's any danger to your precious tree."

The Ninth One's eyes flashed red beyond scarlet. "You know about the Tree?"

"Um, well, not exactly," the Brit said. "I mean, there are rumors floating around, whispers in the depths and heights."

Chapter 36

The two priests decided to spend the night in Mother Heron's cabin rather than attempting to paddle upstream in the gatorous dark. Father Pierre, despite his pain, was in good spirits because everyone had agreed to serve on the Spiritual Warfare Committee. He was also thankful that the river hadn't destroyed his phone, so he could call the bishop.

"Wake up, boss."

"Pierre? Is that you? The signal is weak."

"Yes."

"Are you back from the Loxahatchee? How did it go?"

"Alligators are not logs."

"Alligators? Did you see one?"

"Many eyes were upon me. And several teeth were upon me."

"Oh, no. Do you need emergency help?"

"I am nearly healed already, and we are enjoying snacks and beverages. Boss, everything is like the miracle. Mother Heron and Father Adam have joined our committee."

"Excellent! I'm sure they will be very helpful, but I'm sorry you ran into trouble out there. I will say a prayer for your leg."

"And I will say a prayer for your toe, where the gout lives. See you tomorrow, boss."

"See you tomorrow. Good night."

And it was a good night. The weather cleared and a thousand winged creatures sang their wilderness psalms, lulling the warriors into mystical dreams, the flora and fauna of Eden whirling inside of the sleepers in the most restful reverie, because Mother Heron's prayers were upon them, and her cabin was one of those places where primordial love ruled both the inner and outer landscapes. It was not a "thin place." It was thick as Genesis.

Chapter 37

A peacock called to the dawning river, delivering a battle cry, and the Loxahatchee pushed gently against the wobbling red canoe as if warning everyone that today was not a good day to die. The warriors regulated their strokes in silence, sometimes holding their paddles dripping above the surface while the canoe fought the current until it stalled and hovered for a moment, caught in the tension between perfect rest and regression.

A rifle barrel poked slightly out of the greenery. It resembled a black and silver eye. Father Adam saw the eye but did not sense any evil because he was actually smiling, thinking about breaking into song.

The black and silver eye hissed, and in that flash of eternity before the bullet hit, Mother Heron was certain that the river was wrong. It was a perfect day to die, especially because the forces that wanted her dead had no idea how a heart aligned with the heavens really works, and how she would become, hidden above the birds beating wings into red sunrise, a greater power for the poor souls struggling on the earth.

Mother Heron, hole through her heart, fell overboard. Blood rose to the surface where she went under, while her companions, panicking in the canoe, did not wait for the first alligator to approach Mother's body before they dove into the dark water to save her.

Chapter 38

A Trauma Hawk helicopter swooped down to a clearing near the river where Mother Heron appeared to be sleeping, face-up in the tall grass, her clothes soaked with water and blood. The two priests were kneeling beside her, praying.

A medic climbed out of the helicopter, shouting, "Were you able to stop the bleeding?"

The warriors continued to pray, one in Latin and one in Creole. Both men wept the words more than spoke them.

And the assassin crept away.

Chapter 39

"Gonna have fun today," Dontey said, driving his friends in a van over the bridge. "Gonna take Palm Beach by storm. I don't know if the rich folks love a brother like me, but I love this island."

Rico laughed at his buddy and turned to the young women in the back. Mia and Joan sat cross-legged on the floor, somewhat comfortable but wobbling with every bump. There were no seats in the back of the van, because the vehicle had been reformed by Dontey's church to haul boxes of supplies to low-income families. "Yo," Rico said, "you girls better hide if we see cops. I'll bet you're on the Most Wanted List."

"Highly unlikely," Mia said. "All we did was jump a bridge."

"Bad girls, bad girls," Dontey sang, and then pretended to scold, "You might have crashed into the water and killed an innocent shark."

"Don't talk about sharks," Rico said, his leg stinging. "If I didn't have such a high threshold for pain, this wound would make me scream."

"Joan could paint you as *The Scream*," Mia said. "Go ahead. Make the face for her."

"Or don't," Joan said. "I have enough bad energy in my head right now."

Over the ocean, wisps of clouds and seagulls were mingling in a heavenly dance, and Dontey said to Joan, "I think the sky is the best inspiration for art. If I were a painter, I'd focus on the sky."

She nodded appreciatively at her good friend. Dontey didn't know about her vow to find the killer. All he knew was that she'd found a body and was going through another dark time. "That's a good idea," Joan said, but did not look up. "Everyone should paint the sky."

Rolling down the road among glamorous luxury cars and limousines, the church van proclaimed, with fiery lettering on both sides: PRIMITIVE HOLY GHOST APOSTLES CHURCH OF PENTECOST AND DELIVERANCE. It was a real head turner, and Dontey smiled when a leggy model pranced out of Gucci and stopped dead in her high-heeled tracks. She stared at the van as if to make it burst into flames.

"Gotta love the island," Dontey said, waving at the angry model, then maneuvering the vehicle into a parking space between a silver Ferrari and a black limousine. He put the van in park and leaped out into the very world of wealth. "Last man to the coffee shop buys the shots."

Limping behind, Rico called out, "Not fair, dude. I've been shark-bit."

"Shake it off, bro. No excuses."

Joan and Mia climbed slowly out and began meandering through a majestic archway toward a labyrinth of shops. The semi-hidden but not secret passageway leading to the coffee shop echoed with yips and yaps. Joan sniffed the air, crinkling her nose against a wafting reek of chlorine. The cleaning crew had just washed away daily waste from pampered yet undiapered puppies that answered the call of nature between Louis Vuitton and Saks Fifth Avenue.

"Check out the mannequin," Mia said, pointing at a window display.

A twig of a woman held a shoulder bag that seemed to be made of snakeskin. The bag was adorned with esoteric symbols that included stars, planets, and combinations of letters from a strange alphabet.

"Real snakeskin?" Joan asked.

"I hope not," Mia said, taking a step back.

"It's hideous," Joan said. Although she liked edgy things, she was repulsed by things that were snaky.

Shunning the mannequin and its eerie bag, the friends walked over to the glass cases on the other side of the passageway. Each case held a pair of gold sandals, backlit with a circle of light as if Valentino's footwear were worthy of halos.

Mia, who loved fine things, was impressed by the best of the best. "Look. They really have a layer of gold leaf. I wonder how much they cost."

"Probably an arm and a leg, and your soul," Joan said.

"Oh, well, that's not a very good bargain. But what do you expect on Palm Beach?"

Laughing, the young women continued up the tropical walkway toward the haunting scent of coffee. Through the large window, they saw Rico and Dontey standing at the bar. Dontey looked preppy as usual in his aqua button-down shirt and khaki shorts, and Rico resembled a beach bum. They were tossing back shots of espresso and high-fiving each other like brothers in a coffee bean fraternity.

"Guys are weird," Mia said.

"Wackos," Joan replied. "They've got four shots lined up on the bar. How can they afford to drink like that?"

"It's half my fault. I give Rico addictive gift cards."

"You've created a caffeine monster."

"Yeah. But the coffee gets him talking."

"Gets him talking? Is that really a problem with Rico?"

Mia began to answer, wanting to tell Joan that she suspected Rico was hiding something, but she decided that conversation could wait. "Let's imbibe, *mon amie*."

"*Je suis* thirsty," Joan answered.

They walked through the door of Bullion Coffee and got in line behind Howard Stern near the glass waterfall. Mia pointed at the rushing water. "Look, it's dirty today."

"Yuck, they should turn it off."

Voodoo jazz oozed out of the overhead speakers, inspiring the patrons to talk more loudly. Joan listened intently to hear if the Palm Beachers would reveal any more clues about Donna Murskey.

At the bar, Rico waved his arms and shouted, "Hey, Freckles, over here! We already ordered your drinks for you!"

Mia paused for a moment and glanced in the opposite direction.

Shaking her head, Joan scolded, "You're such a tease."

"No, I'm not a tease. I just don't answer instantly to being called Freckles."

"Good call."

The girls wandered around for a few minutes, riffling through the magazine rack and daily newspapers, and eventually joined the guys at the bar. It was a perfect vantage point to observe the new blood and bluebloods entering the shop, the celebrities already in line, and the shady people in the leather chairs by the waterfall.

"Gotta pee," Rico said.

"You need to hold your beans better," Dontey chided. "We just got here, and there's a lot more to drink."

"It's that waterfall. It talks to my bladder, and my stupid bladder listens."

"Fine," Mia said, interrupting the deeply meaningful conversation. "Go pee."

"Okay, but don't discuss anything important or anything funny," Rico said, rushing away. "In fact, don't talk about anything until you hear the flush."

Rolling her eyes, Joan murmured to Mia, "That's your guy."

"He can't help it," she said defensively. "It's the waterfall's fault. Right, Dontey?"

"Look at the front of the line," Dontey said, intrigued by a man complaining at the cash register. "What a wannabe."

The Saks-dressed man was angry about the price of cashews. "Are you freaking kidding? Are you freaking *kidding me*?"

"This is good stuff," Dontey said.

The barista spoke with a friendly calm. "Sir, would you like to purchase the cashews, or should I put them back for you?"

"Three dollars? For a few lousy nuts?"

"He's nuts," Dontey said, grinning. "This is awesome. I love watching spoiled people."

"Three dollars, sir."

"Listen, missy. Let me tell you something. I didn't get where I am by paying top dollar for healthy snacks."

The barista was not particularly interested in the story of the man's rise to fortune. "Would you like for me to put the item back for you?"

"You can put it—"

FLUSH!

The toilet in the coffee shop was among the most powerful in the world, and the sound was like a tidal wave crashing through the walls. Rico reappeared, limping past the waterfall without making eye contact with its mesmerizing waters. At that moment, the Saks man stormed out of the store, with no coffee and no cashews. All he had was his pride and a proclamation: "From now on, I will exchange my currency for the goods and services of Mr. Schultz!"

Rico rejoined his friends, standing between Mia and Dontey. "Did you know," he asked, "that the dude of Starbucks is the same dude that wrote the *Peanuts* comic strip?"

"You're confused," Joan said, shaking her purple head. "You're very confused."

"Yeah," Rico said. "Schultz invented Snoopy and Starbucks. Up in Fork, Washington."

Mia sipped her drink. "Sweetie, I think you're talking about two different people. Or maybe three."

"No, I read about it on Facebook. Schultz invented all sorts of things, including—"

"Stephen King," Dontey said.

"Really? Schultz invented Stephen King?"

"Bro, look at the guy who just cut in line. That's Stephen King."

All four teenagers stared, along with several other patrons, and Rico tried to be the loud voice of reason. "No, that's not him. Stephen King rides around in one of those super-cool talking wheelchairs."

"You mean Stephen Hawking," Mia said, wondering if perhaps a shark had eaten part of Rico's brain.

The creepy guy in the front of the line smiled maniacally and raised his fingers to resemble devil horns.

"I hate that sign," Dontey said. "Even if it's a joke, it's like sending an open invitation into hell."

"I'd like his autograph," Mia announced. "I wonder if he'd be angry if I politely asked. According to *Publisher's Weekly*, King has sold more books than Hemingway and Faulkner combined. Oh my gosh, here he comes."

"Hello, ladies," he said, flashing a wicked grin. "And hello, gents."

Rico exclaimed, "You're the dude who directed *The Shining*! I knew it!"

The author's eyes grew wide. "Wow, you must have telekinetic powers. Please don't focus your powerful mind on me, Ricardo. I might not survive. I might become a ghoul and rattle your window every night."

Dontey whispered to Mia, "How did he know Rico's name?"

"I don't know," Mia said. "That's weird. And King is acting weird in general. He's known to be shy and withdrawn. Maybe he only acts like one of his characters when he visits Palm Beach."

Rico reached out to shake the guy's hand, and then withdrew it and began limping away. "I gotta go. Sorry. It's the waterfall."

The barista appeared at the end of the bar, pretending to be undead, her eyes wide and lifeless. "Here is your drink, Mr. King. Thank you, and haunt again."

"Mmm," he said, "very tasty demon bile. Yum."

Mia giggled with admiration while Joan slipped away from the group. The tormented artist was in a real horror story and didn't need any help from a master of nightmares. With none of her friends noticing, Joan took her drink and headed toward the exit, and was stopped cold by a familiar voice.

"Hello, friend," the voice said.

Joan turned and saw the handsome man in the corner. He was wearing his amazing hair and perfectly pressed green suit. He hadn't been there a minute ago, and it was like he'd simply appeared out of nowhere. The girl's first thought was to run away, her muscles tensing and heart pounding. However, as if mystically drawn to the man, Joan shuffled over to his table. The guy smiled in a way that showed he was aware of her discomfort. "Please. Sit down next to me."

Joan hesitated, thinking about running for the door, and then she sat and took a nervous sip of coffee. "So. We meet again."

"Yes," Mr. Handsome said, winking down at his phone. "I just left a message for you."

"I don't think so. My phone never rang."

"It's an important message."

Giving him a prickly stare, Joan replied, "That's what all the boys say."

He chuckled, syncopated to the beat of the voodoo music. "I am not a boy."

"Oh? What are you?"

"More of a guardian angel. If . . ."

"If what?"

"If you will allow yourself to be guarded."

Gulping her coffee, Joan said, "I realize I'm in danger, but I don't care. I'm not sure if you'd understand this, but I have a mission to accomplish."

The guy nodded and lifted his phone. "Look. Do you recognize the painting?"

Joan's eyes narrowed. "That's my painting. *Adam and Eve in Paradise*. What's it doing on your phone?"

"Never mind how it got there. Who is the girl in the painting?"

Joan studied the sad eyes that gave the face its soulfulness. "She's just a girl I made up. She isn't anybody I know. The girl just appeared in my mind, and I gave her life. Do you think she's beautiful?"

Mr. Handsome nodded. "Very beautiful. I think she's Donna Murskey."

"What? No. Are you sure?"

"I'm sure."

"But I never met her. I never saw a photograph or anything."

"Yes, well, her image is your likeness." Handsome pointed a scarred finger at the screen. "What is the redness on her belly?"

"Redness on her belly?"

"Yes. Like a knife wound."

Joan hesitated. "I think you're imagining that."

Laughing without mirth, the guy said, "Am I imagining that the boy in the painting is Rico?"

"I don't know. He might resemble Rico. But he's just . . . nobody. I made him up. I made up the boy and the girl. They're just symbols."

"Symbols?"

"Of love."

"That's nonsense, Joan. There are no symbols. Everything is real. Everything *is*. Listen, Joan. Are you listening to the magic that *IS*?"

Glancing over her shoulder, she answered, "I feel like you're going to tell me something horrible."

Handsome leaned close, so close that his hair tickled Joan's ear, and he slowly whispered, "A powerful man has seen your painting.

He thinks you have a spiritual gift, a sense of premonition. And he thinks you know who killed Donna."

"What?"

"He believes you're a witch. Or a high priestess."

Joan tried to laugh. "Does this powerful man want to burn me at the stake?"

"No. He doesn't want to burn your flesh. He wants to buy it, and devour it."

Chapter 40

Adjacent to the cathedral was a small chapel where the bishop spent every morning from seven until eight, all alone and sometimes in agony, and he was startled, at exactly 7:46, when a candle suddenly danced and flickered out. That was followed by a knock, a sort of hollow rap-rap-rap, like somebody was tapping at the door with a bone.

"Hello?"

The bishop's hello was not an invitation, more of a request for information, but the door suddenly creaked open a little, and a triangle of light appeared in the chapel.

"Hello? Who's there?"

The door opened wider, and the bishop saw a shrouded, humanlike figure.

"Mrs. Teffler?"

The shrouded figure remained outside, haloed by the harsh light. "I am not Mrs. Teffler."

"Who are you then?"

"I am Beauchamp."

"Detective?"

Beauchamp leaned in slightly and whispered, "There have been possible developments in the Murskey case."

"Developments?"

"Yes. Two of your priests are downtown at this moment, giving statements about another murder."

The bishop paused, wondering if he should keep silent. "Two of my priests are suspects? They're suspected of murder?"

"Witnesses," the detective assured him. "Father Pierre and Father Adam are witnesses. But they didn't actually see the killer."

"And . . . Mother Heron?"

"Dead."

The bishop bowed his head. "Lord have mercy. Do you know who did the killing?"

Beauchamp pushed the door wide open, and a blazing brightness entered the chapel as if to devour it. "Maybe you could tell me, Bishop. I think you know."

Chapter 41

On the north side of Apocalypse Island, the WINGS had an underground haunt, a private clubhouse where they gathered in a circle around a stolen red phone. Dapper in golf attire and tribal masks, the men reveled in their obscene wealth. One owned banks, another weapons, another porn, another pharmaceuticals, another technology, another oil, another agriculture, another media, and the Ninth One owned them all. Wearing a scarlet mask, he stood while the others sat, and gave a report on what was happening with "The Everglades Restoration Project," a code phrase for the progress of the Tree of the Knowledge of Good and Evil.

"It seems to have reached maturity," the Ninth One said, his voice rising. "We paid dearly for the seed and for the means to keep the Tree hidden in plain sight. And now the enlightening fruits are ripening—for the feast of all feasts."

The WINGS erupted with applause.

"Hell yeah!" Weapons yelled, his arms shooting out with open palms. "I want payback for the billion I kicked in!"

Yuck, yuck, yuck, yuck, yuck, yuck, yuck, yuck, the men laughed and boasted about their contributions to the project and how they'd live in the full knowledge of pleasure, luxury, and power in the kingdom at hand.

Porn fidgeted, unable to control himself, and finally asked, "What about the new virgin? Is she ready to be touched?"

The Ninth One frowned behind his grinning mask. "Joan will not be easy for us to touch." He paused, hating to hear or say the girl's name, and then his eyes were like fire. "However, she will be easy to sacrifice."

Chapter 42

"Viva La Vida" rang out on Joan's phone. It was a song that she'd listened to constantly after her father was killed. The melody now struck the girl with so much melancholy that it gave her pause—as if a few notes of music could conjure absolute dread—and she took the call.

"Hello?" she said, stepping away from the man in green.

"Why were you talking to the guy in the corner?"

"What?"

"That handsome devil only lies."

Joan hurried out the door of the coffee shop. "What? Who is this?" She hated talking on the phone in public and tried to find privacy behind a giant pot of orange flowers.

"Mr. Hair is not your friend." The voice emanated from both the device and the air, as if someone were both phoning and calling down from the balcony. "He has friends in low places, the very lowest of places, and he's trying to drag you down."

"Is that you, Detective? I'm hearing double. Where are you?"

"Up here," the voice said. "You were just looking at me."

The girl stared heavenward, and there, among the vines on the balcony, was Beauchamp with his white raincoat fluttering in the wind. He looked like an angel—a very perturbed angel. "Don't look at me. But listen. We need to talk about the WINGS. Meet me up higher, above the parking ramp."

"What?"

"Meet me on the roof."

"Why?"

"Because it's important, Joan. Don't ride the elevator. Don't take the stairs. Walk up the incline."

"No," she said. "I don't think so."

"No? You don't want to talk about Donna? It's all over the Internet that you made a vow to find her killer."

Joan raised her voice. "All over the Internet? I sent one tweet."

Several shoppers turned their well-groomed heads toward the giant pot of apparently talking flowers. "I'm not saying another word," Joan said.

"Meet me on the roof. Now."

The white coat flashed away from the balcony, and the girl stayed hidden behind the flowers for a while, gathering her thoughts. Eventually, Joan discerned that it was best to obey him. She marched over to the incline of the parking ramp, where the ascent to the roof was like a spiral staircase for expensive cars, and Joan began winding her way up, the sound of her boots echoing against the walls. Halfway to the top, she paused, thinking how easy it might be for a dark sedan with a trained assassin to run her over. Would she just stand there and raise her hands to her face like *The Scream*? Or would she leap in the air and smash her boots through the windshield? Joan would not find out at that time, because there wasn't any traffic in the ramp, just a lot of exercise—march, march, march—all the way to the sun-bleached top.

Beauchamp was already at the far end, leaning precariously over the ledge. "Come here," he said, "look at this."

When the girl got closer, but not all the way to the ledge, the detective uttered, "What a world. Look at this, and consider all the wealth and power."

Joan didn't think much about wealth and power, but she leaned over the edge to admire the Spanish architecture of the nearby Everglades Club, designed by the world-famous Addison Mizner. And over on the mainland, the symmetry of the twin towers of Trump Plaza gave structure to the horizon, and a tall black bank known as "The Goth Vader" arose in the north. Below the bank were shiny yachts, floating like dreams in the sky-reflecting waterway. The girl squinted and tried to see the art museum, but it was hidden behind palm trees and condos.

The detective stared out west toward the corporate farms flowing with fruits, vegetables, and sugar cane all the way to the Everglades. "Listen to me, Joan. The crimes on this earth are becoming less natural, more supernatural, and you mustn't get caught in the middle. Like Donna, you're not strong enough to survive."

Joan felt like telling off the detective, but she kept her composure and calmly stated, "I'm already in the middle. I'm already surviving."

"You should flee this place," Beauchamp said. "Go to Savannah and study art. Go take a summer class, and don't come back."

There was real concern in the detective's voice, and yet Joan felt violated. How did he know about her plan to move to Savannah? Joan lurched away from him, striding toward the spiral descent of the ramp. The girl could feel the detective's gaze on her back—could actually feel it reaching inside toward her heart—and she thought: *How dare he? Is he getting some sick pleasure from watching me?*

A fatherly voice called out, "Joan. Stop. Look out over the ocean."

The girl quickened her pace, thinking: *No, I won't stop. No, I won't look at the ocean.*

Down the snaking exit and into the shadows, Joan marched away, thinking the detective was nothing but a creep bent on making her life miserable.

He doesn't care about me, she thought, descending. *And he doesn't care about Donna.*

If Joan had gone to the east side of the roof and looked out over the ocean, she would have seen something whirling at the horizon. It was like a circle of ashes, but not from a fire, something otherworldly (dismissed by the local meteorologists as a rather insignificant anomaly) that would culminate, in three days, into a killer storm.

Chapter 43

Before she was murdered, Donna Murskey sent a secret email.

Thanks for finding that place up north that helps with adoption and everything. The nun on the phone sounded like she understood my situation. I told her that she couldn't understand everything because of what I've seen. She said she had secrets, too, but I'm not sure I can trust her yet. Isn't that sad? I don't even quite trust nuns.

The men who hate me twisted what was already wrong in my head and said I was a goddess, but that didn't mean anything as far as respect. What good is a goddess that's a hunk of meat? And they filled my head with so many chemicals. Sometimes it seemed like a real life, I mean it was more intense than the usual and I'd be lying if I said I didn't enjoy some of it. My body and mind craved experiences beyond the norm and there were times when I thought I was the lucky girl.

You tried to pull me out of hell. You even said prayers for me. I have to admit I liked your kiss more than your prayers.

The baby has the cutest little kick. A tiny knock-knock in my tummy.

Knock-knock, the baby says.

Who's there?

I'm here, mommy. I don't care how I got here. I love you.

I love you too, baby.

The men said I can't name him because "he will be greater than a name." Who talks like that? They said if I ate all the good and evil, then my son would be "the prince beyond peace." Everything they said was riddles and crap. They have no idea how stupid they are. Always acting in public like they're the good ones of the world. They hide behind their money, and they do hideous things in the dark.

After I told them, "I won't eat of the tree," I snuck back to my parents' house and lay awake all night. I'd seen the ocean a thousand times and never really cared, but in the morning I saw a man in a rowboat. He was fishing and the sunrise turned the water into a golden chalice. The fisherman was in the middle of the cup like he'd been caught and God was about to swallow him up.

*I cried all that morning. I wanted to call you and tell you about the Everglades island, because I knew you'd believe me. But I didn't call, because I didn't want you to insist on seeing me. One more of your kisses, and I might have stayed. And that would have been too dangerous, especially for the baby. R, if you're reading this message, show it to someone that you trust. Here is the **link** with directions to the Tree. It's all real. But don't go there. Please don't go there, ok?*

That's it. Except, you want to know something else for real? I think I love you. But I know you're taken. So let's just leave it at that.

—Donna

Chapter 44

Deep in the Everglades, on an island with the perfect soil and the perfect amount of light and shade, the WINGS planted the last remaining seed from the Tree of the Knowledge of Good and Evil. A protective moat surrounded the island: muck-colored water eight feet deep and swarming with eels, water snakes, and alligators. High-tech surveillance also surrounded the paradise, preventing any trespasser from stumbling upon the site.

The WINGS had grown the Tree by buying the services of the most adept botanist in the world, a wizened old man known as the Babylonian, who could manipulate the ancient seed without causing lightning strikes or other destruction. During the process of tilling and planting, the WINGS immersed the Babylonian in dark rituals, and when the seed of Eden sprouted and the sapling became a tree, the botanist was given his reward.

The WINGS lifted the Babylonian on their shoulders and hailed him as the "Grand Master Gardener of the World," and cheered and sang his praises and dumped him into the moat, where he was eaten by eels, snakes, and alligators.

Dissention then arose among the WINGS, because the Tree stopped growing and would not bear fruit. There were murmurings, accusations, and veiled threats among the powers and principalities. The WINGS began to unravel, suspecting a conspiracy among the conspirators, and divergent instructions were given to the snipers who crawled among the serpents. Weapons wanted everyone shot on sight, immediately, while Media wanted more cameras installed, and Banks claimed that he'd never believed in the seed to begin with. "We should have spent the money on robots with pig DNA," he whined. "Robots and swine were my idea. I'm on record with that investment advice. Check your monthly statements." And so the Ninth One tried to ease tensions and reconcile Weapons to Porn, and Oil to Media, Pharmaceuticals to Technology, and Agriculture to Banks.

When the Halloween negotiations got overly heated, the Ninth One visited the island alone, and sat near the Tree, and chanted to spite all tongues. Wearing an alternate face, he sang praises to the metaphysical rebels, praises to the gods that such men and women became, praises to the willfulness of every soul and spirit that would murder the heavens and "Do as thou wilt."

The Tree started growing again, and by Christmas was higher than the height of a man on the shoulders of a giant. Feeling merrily all-powerful, the Ninth One watched a rat snake slither up the trunk to the lowest branch and flick its tongue at buds that seemed brighter than sunlight.

"Do not eat of the Tree," the man said. "Only the WINGS are welcome to the feast."

The rat snake flicked its tongue and recoiled as if struck by lightning. Looking up through the branches, the dying snake saw eyes. The eyes of a dragon.

Chapter 45

Mr. Handsome answered on the first ring. "Hello, my friend. I knew you'd call."

Stomping away from the parking ramp, Joan asked, "Are you still in Bullion?"

"Yes. Your friends are here, too. Your blonde friend just let Stephen King sign an autograph on her foot."

"She did what?"

"Yes, she took off her sandal and let the guy scribble his name, or some sort of omen or curse."

Joan shook her head, feeling a mess of mixed emotions. The whole world seemed absurd, and yet her heart ached for truth. She leaned against a Gucci window display, another snakeskin purse. "What more can you tell me about Donna Murskey?"

"I have nothing to report," the guy said. "There are people listening and cameras watching, so you and I should meet in secret."

"There's a police station nearby," the girl said, not even trying to hide the snark. "Let's have our chat there."

There was a long silence, and Joan thought the call was over.

"Here's a better idea," Handsome finally said. "Let's go to my apartment."

"No. That's not a good place."

"You're right, Joan. It's not a good place. I mean, it's haunted."

"Hmm," the girl replied, "do you have cats?"

"My apartment is not haunted by cats. It's haunted by nine spirits."

"Exactly. Cats."

"Well, to be honest, Joan. I am more of a bird person than a cat person, although my favorite animal is the bear that dances alone in the mountainous woods."

The man's voice was so gypsy-like, musical, and timeless, that she suddenly asked him, "How old are you? For real. Listen, I don't go to the apartments of older men."

"I'm twenty-nine."

"Ancient."

"Ancient? No. More like prime."

"Whatever. I don't even know your name."

"It's Seth."

"Okay, ancient Seth. Let's meet in a neutral location."

"There's no such thing as a neutral location. You know that. The whole world is occupied territory, including my apartment."

"It's probably a war zone of laundry and dirty dishes."

"Listen, Joan Dior. Do you know where I live?"

"A nursing home?"

"Very funny. You'll be twenty-nine in a heartbeat. Life happens fast."

Joan thought about Donna and how she never got past her teens. The image of the poor girl in the lagoon brought a lump to Joan's throat. "Seth, if you have information about Donna, don't play games. Just tell me."

"I will. In my apartment."

"Why there?"

"Because my apartment overlooks a beautiful garden."

A beautiful garden was one of Joan's favorite phrases and an image that suggests the joy of eternity, and yet she felt a sudden chill in the sweltering air.

Seth continued, boasting, "My place overlooks Gateway Sculpture Garden."

"Where they host the Demon Dance?"

"Yes. Do you know about that dance?"

A surge of disgust filled Joan's body, and she felt the urge to run toward the ocean. She understood why Rico had wanted to float away for a while, hoping to end up closer to the sky than the depths. Joan wanted to kick off her combat boots and drift on the peaceful water, and yet the girl stood still, ready for whatever. "All right, Seth. I'll speak with you at your apartment."

"Good. Can you go now?"

"Yeah, but you'll have to drive me. I'm standing outside of Gucci, near a van that says PRIMITIVE HOLY GHOST APOSTLES CHURCH OF PENTECOST AND DELIVERANCE. You can't miss it."

"I'm already here," Seth said, sneaking up beside her.

She gave him a threatening look. "Don't do that."

"Do what?"

"Don't appear out of nowhere. That's how people get shot."

Seth laughed. "Do you have a gun?"

"That's for me to know and you to find out."

He chuckled. "You don't even carry a skinny purse to complement those skinny jeans. You're not a fighter, Joan. You're a lover."

Joan looked him steadily in the eye. "Actually, I'm an artist, Seth. And there's nothing more dangerous."

Chapter 46

The bishop's office was silent as a graveyard, except for the sipping of coffee and the crunching of cookies. The members of the Spiritual Warfare Committee huddled in a circle of folding chairs, with Mrs. Teffler as the focal point, wearing her Sunday dress covered with peacocks that proclaimed, "Yes, I am the prettiest prayer warrior. And do you see all these eyes? Nothing escapes me. I am one of the few. The proud. The church secretaries."

Each member of the committee was anxious, and showing it in a different way.

Father Adam scratched his crown of white hair, yawned, and then reached down for a cigarette, thinking it was time for a smoke break.

Father Pierre rubbed his wounded leg, his eyes teary with thoughts of Mother Heron.

The bishop tried to offer a continuous smile, despite fretting about the scandal, murder, and demon possession in his diocese. He rubbed his sore temples and thought, *Well, there's still a chance I might become a cardinal.*

Phone balanced on one knee, Lil Reynolds had a notebook on the other and recorded everything. So far, it was merely the sipping of coffee and crunching of cookies.

"I overcooked them," Mrs. Teffler confessed. "I got distracted by a buzzing helicopter."

"I am the one for overcooked cookies," Father Pierre said, trying to make her feel better. "I am the one for seconds."

"They're fine," Father Adam said, thinking the nearly burned cookies would taste better with a smoke.

Lil hadn't tried a cookie, and she wished the weak coffee would turn into *café con leche.* "Shall we get started?"

Giving her a nasty glance, Mrs. Teffler responded, "Committees usually engage in fellowship before conducting business."

Lil returned the gaze, and the retired exorcist remembered why he hated committees so much. He cleared his charred throat and said, "C'mon, folks, let's get serious and ask the archangel to defend us in battle."

Four of the members prayed while Lil remained silent and studied the fervent faces. How could they believe this archaic stuff? How could they believe that a warrior spirit was really listening to them and would be moved to action? To her ears, the prayers sounded like mumbo jumbo or jumbo mumbo or jumbo jumbo, and she began thinking about the many hours she'd spent in church and how the "magic" never worked on her, despite some real effort, especially during Lent when she'd given up coffee (as a child) and boys (as a teenager). Eventually, Lil became one of those people who exchanged the church altar for the open sky, believing that the universe was godless but a friend that would give her everything, including an endless supply of coffee and boys.

Jumbo mumbo mumbo, she heard the committee pray. Weary of their repeated words, Lil guzzled an entire cup of coffee. The weak brew went down wrong, and the reporter gagged, convulsed, and spewed.

"Crap!"

Lil didn't say that. Cranky Pants said it, because she'd spewed on his pants.

"Crap!"

Lil said it that time, and after dabbing a few napkins here and there, she decided to take over the meeting. "Listen to me," she said. "Perhaps it makes sense for you folks to repeat the same old prayers, over and over again, but we have serious issues to discuss. Bish, do you have any updates about Donna or Mother Heron? Have you spoken to Beauchamp today? We need real information. I mean, how many *Our Fathers* does the universe need to hear? And isn't Michael the Archangel already on the job? Isn't he already commanding his army? Call me a skeptic and you'd be right, but do you really need so much repetition?"

Mrs. Teffler gave Lil a look that could slay a demon. "Are you really against repetition? What about the repeating sunrise and sunset? What about the rise and fall of the tides? And the blooming of trees? Think about the repetition of Christmas and your favorite hymns and the recurrent singing of *Happy Birthday*. Listen, Miss Writer, and remember this: all of the glorious things in life are worth repeating."

"Time for a smoke break," Father Adam said. "And a fresh cup of coffee. Is that okay with you, Bishop?"

"Yes, good idea," he said. "I just have a few announcements to make before we—"

"Discuss some issues," Lil said, interrupting. "We need to discuss some issues regarding the murders. Remember the murders? In my humble heretic opinion, I think that's why we're really here."

With a pained expression, the bishop turned toward the wall and the painting of Michael glowing above a candle. The great angel was contemplating the glory of Heaven, in perfect repose, while plunging a sword into the belly of the Beast.

"Time for a smoke break," the bishop announced.

Nodding and smiling, Father Pierre said, "My smoke will be the cup of water."

The reporter smirked and scribbled in her notebook. "*My smoke will be the cup of water.*"

Mrs. Teffler lurched out of her chair. "I'll get more cookies—for those that appreciate them."

The Haitian followed her, limping toward the kitchen while Father Adam went outside for a Lucky Strike. Lil and the bishop stayed in their chairs, the former scribbling while the latter closed his eyes and moved his lips with what seemed to be more mumbo jumbo. After a few minutes, Lil began giggling. "This. Is. Ridiculous."

Opening an eye, he responded, "What's ridiculous?"

Lil pointed at the circle of battered, coffee-stained chairs. "Do you actually believe this is the way to conduct spiritual warfare? How could the devils take this seriously? Do you think your prayers can fly beyond these walls and actually help someone in the real world?"

Opening his other eye, the bishop said, "We seem mundane, and perhaps even foolish. I know. All of us have serious flaws. Father Adam can barely make it twenty minutes before his hands start shaking from nicotine withdrawal. Mrs. Teffler has anger issues."

"You think?"

"I think we all need grace. Father Pierre is probably the best of us, and perhaps we should follow his example."

"He seems childlike."

"Yes, and he's brilliant. Father has published articles on metaphysics that would make your head spin."

Turning her neck as if getting the kinks out, Lil said, "This whole thing makes my head spin. I mean, really, considering what we know about science and technology, isn't it time to accept the fact that God passed away during the Renaissance? Or maybe didn't pass away. He simply became irrelevant. Fact is, most people just want to get rich and have fun. Because life is boring, and then you die."

Mrs. Teffler returned with fresh coffee. "I sweetened it with milk and honey," she said, handing a cup to Lil.

"No thank you," the reporter said, grabbing her phone and hitting the record button. "The Spiritual Warfare Committee is now indulging in bad coffee, cookies, and cigarettes. I'm sure the hordes of the underworld are trembling with fear. Or maybe roaring with laughter."

"Why, you b—"

"Hush, Mrs. Teffler," the bishop said.

"But she's mocking us."

"Yes. And how should we respond?"

Huffing and puffing, the old receptionist walked out of the room. "If anyone wants me, I'll be outside smoking with the exorcist."

Chapter 47

"It's really haunted," Seth explained, gesturing toward the acre of wild and yet manicured jungle. "I love living here, despite the killer rent. And look, the garden has a sinkhole—it seems to go down forever—but I can still give you a tour."

"I don't care about the garden," Joan said, feeling uneasy about being in the realm of the Demon Dance. "Tell me more about Donna. You promised to tell me everything."

"I will enlighten you," Seth said, striding down the sidewalk. "Follow me."

The moldy walkway was bordered by century plants, a benign name for a species of flora resembling saw blades tipped with long thin daggers. A sudden gust of wind shoved the plants forward, poking Joan in the arm. The girl's blood rose like a red bulb until it burst and trickled down to her wrist, but she didn't cry out. Her thoughts were with Donna. With every step toward Seth's apartment, she felt closer to the murdered girl.

The bloodletting plants became a wall of twisted trees, drooping with fruit and littering the ground with the remains of dozens of smashed mangoes, the juices blotched together in a coagulated mess.

"The rats have a feast every night," Seth said. "But you'll be gone by then. Here are the stairs to my apartment."

The building was nearly black, perhaps two centuries old, much higher than it was wide, like a huge vertical coffin rising from the ground.

Joan slowly climbed the creaking stairs while the words echoed in her head: *The rats have a feast every night. But you'll be gone by then.*

Chapter 48

Future soldiers like Rico tend to have many fine qualities, including bravery, earnestness, and tenacity, but they typically lack patience for novelists who autograph the feet of their girlfriends. The moment that Mia put her cami sandal back on, Rico grabbed her by the hand and yanked her out of the coffee shop.

Mia thought Rico was taking her to the beach to find Joan, so she didn't protest too much about being removed from the presence of a celebrity. "I hope to see him again," she said. "He's quirky and fun."

"Could you be a little less obvious about how much you're into him?"

Mia freed her hand. "What's that supposed to mean?"

"You let him sign your foot. That's weird."

"It's just ink, Rico. It'll wash away."

"What if it doesn't wash away? What if it's permanent?"

"It's not permanent. It will be gone tonight. Or tomorrow. Okay?"

Rico didn't like the idea of Mia sleeping with King's eerie scribble, but he wouldn't be a total jerk and demand that she scrub it off immediately, especially since he was known to go a day or two without bathing. "Okay," he said with a forgiving smile. And he tried to use psychology instead of making a demand. "Let's check out the beach, and maybe wade in the water a little. And, um, clean our feet."

Mia gave him a punch on the shoulder. And the couple meandered through the labyrinth of high fashion and jewelry, making their way past the shade of the spiral parking ramp and into the fiery light near Ocean Avenue. There they paused, sharing a kiss while waiting for a line of luxury cars and limos. Eventually, the young lovers crossed over to the ivory tower, a recent addition to the town, built to resemble an ancient edifice from the Mediterranean. Rico and Mia stood in partial shade, and the girl scanned the shoreline for signs of camouflage. "I don't see Joan anywhere. I'll text her."

"Maybe she went shopping."

"Shopping? I don't think so. Not on Palm Beach. She'll text me right back, I'm sure."

"Cool."

The couple was silent for a while, just looking at the ocean with its triptych of weather. To the north was deep-blue sky over aquamarine, dotted with small white clouds and boats. And down south, the water rippled with gold, a pirate's dream all the way to the Keys. And in the middle was a mysterious haze, a hint of both cloud and clearing, the outer edge forming something like a ring.

Rico wrapped his arm around Mia's waist, thinking that would help their conversation, but she freed herself from his grasp and uttered a sigh. "I want to see Stephen King again. I want to ask him something about *The Stand*."

"I liked that movie," Rico said, still feeling jealous but trying to connect. "The best part was when they walked through the swamp and got covered by bloodsuckers."

Shaking her head, Mia said, "That's *Stand by Me*. That's totally different."

"Are you sure?"

"Yeah, I'm sure. *Stand by Me* is a coming-of-age story. *The Stand* is about the battle between Good and Evil."

"Dang," Rico muttered. "I was hoping we were talking about the same thing for a change."

"For a change? What's that supposed to mean?"

"Nothing." He closed his eyes to Mia and the multi-faced ocean. "Absolutely nothing."

After a minute of silence, during which Mia thought about sneaking away, she reached over and touched the side of his face.

"Open your eyes, Rico. Talk to me. You've been acting strange for months. What's going on?"

His lids fluttered open, but Rico avoided the questioning face. He looked at the hazy ring in the sky, took a deep breath of salty air, and slowly exhaled. "I have something to say, but it's not good. I should have told you a long time ago. I almost told you at prom, but it would've ruined your night."

Dying to know what almost ruined her prom, Mia positioned herself between Rico and the ocean, claiming his direct line of sight. "Tell me. Whatever it is, Rico, I'd rather know than be in the dark."

A gray helicopter buzzed along the shoreline, casting a quick shadow that seemed to be eating a line in the sand. The helicopter gave Rico a terrible feeling, but he was already in a world of hurt. He said, "I did something I shouldn't have done."

"Rico, we've all done things we shouldn't have," Mia replied, hoping the revelation didn't involve her, or rather did not involve them. "Whatever you did, just make amends and move forward. Most things can be fixed."

"Not this."

"Tell me."

"I kissed Donna Murskey."

The buzz of the copter died beneath crashing waves and laughing children. Mia pretended that she hadn't been able to hear his words. "What? What did you say?"

"I didn't mean to kiss her. It just happened."

Mia collapsed against the seawall, yet refused to cry, while Rico continued to explain. "We were at a party together. The richest guy on the island had a crazy party."

"A party? You never mentioned that. Who goes to a party on Palm Beach and doesn't mention it?"

"Well, I kept quiet because I know how much you like mansions and things. I knew you'd want to go with me, but—"

"What?"

Grasping her hand, hoping that would make her feel wanted, Rico said slowly, "But you weren't invited."

Mia flung aside his hand as if it were a snake. "I'm done talking about this. I'm going back to Stephen King."

"Seriously, don't do that. He's evil."

"Yeah? And what are you?"

"I'm sorry, Mia. I'm really sorry. What I did was wrong, but I don't think it was evil. I got caught up in the moment, trying to make Donna feel better about herself."

Glaring, Mia answered with a scorching voice, "Did she feel better about herself? Is that why Donna's dead? Seriously, I'm out of here."

"Hey, be careful. Watch out for traffic!"

Rico watched in horror while Mia rushed across the busy street, barely avoiding a long, black hearse. He called after her, "You don't think I hurt Donna, do you?"

I don't know, the girl thought, angrily weeping her way down the golden avenue. *I don't know.*

Chapter 49

Seth's apartment was a dwelling of light. Paintings of celestial scenes colored the blue walls from floor to ceiling—heavens in every direction—and skylights flooded the abode with a wild illumination that bordered on oppressive.

"Welcome to the haunted heights," he said proudly, leading Joan to a window overlooking the garden.

The girl was not interested in scenery. She was focused on finding out what the guy knew about ritual murder. And yet Joan couldn't help herself—she glanced through the window to admire the artistic jungle.

"Yes, a visionary's dream," Seth said. "Do you wish it was yours?"

Beneath the nearest palm was a big lizard with a sticky tongue hunting bugs and slurping them down to their doom. Joan looked away and pointed to the far side of the garden. "What's that huge stone door?"

Seth leaned over and nestled his face close to Joan's. His touch caused her to flinch, but she stayed close to him, hoping her tolerance would pay off. He whispered, "You are attracted to the Gateway. It happens to every girl who looks out this window. She sees the open door, like it's something from an adventure movie, and she begs for a tour. And what can I do? I give her a tour through the Gateway to Hell."

"Hmm," Joan said, not showing fear or interest but merely appraising the merits of the sculpture. "Hmm. You'd think the Gateway to Hell would be leading down to another place. Instead, it merely leads horizontally from one section of the garden to another."

Seth whispered directly into the girl's ear. "I don't think it's a matter of direction as much as a matter of the will."

His breath was sweet, and yet Joan was repulsed. "What do you mean—the will?"

"Last year, at the Demon Dance, Donna whirled through the Gateway. It was her choice."

"Her choice?" Joan paused, trying to think of a defense for the dead girl. "Was she paid to dance?"

Seth nodded. "She was paid for everything."

"She was manipulated," Joan said, noticing a circle beyond the Gateway. "Donna didn't know the whole story. She was simply being alive, and making mistakes, like most kids."

"Or maybe it wasn't a mistake," Seth said. "Maybe it's good and right to dance for the owners of the earth. If you stay here for an hour, I can introduce you to a real power."

"A real power? You mean someone in the WINGS?"

Seth's eyes were affirmative, and perhaps full of lies.

Joan had more questions for him, but just then her phone rang, and she said, "I need to get this."

The raven-haired neo-gypsy, or whoever he was, stepped away to be polite, and then listened to every word.

"Hey, Mia, what's up?"

"Joan, where'd you disappear to? I've been trying to get a hold of you."

"I'm over in West Palm."

"Don't tell me you freaked out and walked over the bridge alone."

"No, I got a ride."

"You didn't Uber, I hope."

"No, I didn't Uber."

"You hitchhiked? That's the easiest way to get abducted. A girl is a thousand times more likely to be abducted while hitchhiking."

"I'm fine," Joan said.

"You don't sound fine. You sound nervous. Are you sure you haven't been abducted? Who are you with? Are you free to speak?"

113

"I'm free to speak, Mia. I'm over at the Gateway Garden, just talking to—"

"Wait a sec. You're at the Gateway Garden? Isn't that where they host the Demon Dance? Joan, please tell me you're not talking to a Demon Dance guy."

"Just a guy, Mia."

"What guy? Did you let some weirdo from Palm Beach give you a ride across the bridge? Say something in code if you want me to call the police. Say something about uncomfortable shoes, and I'll immediately call the cops."

"Mia, why are you freaking out?"

"I'm worried about you, Joan. You've been through hell—not everyone finds a dead body—and now I'm afraid you're obsessed. Do you remember my speech about obsession? It's a gateway to mental illness."

Joan glanced over her shoulder to check on Seth. He seemed distracted by a large cockroach scurrying under a tattered loveseat. "What about you, Mia? You sound upset. Should I be worried?"

"I'm worried about you being in a garden with a creeper."

"I'm above the garden, not in it."

"Above it? In a tree? In a helicopter? What do you mean?"

"An upstairs apartment."

"Are you crazy, Joan? You can't go into strange apartments. Say something in code about high heels and I'll call nine-one-one."

"I'm fine," Joan whispered. "Trust me. I've got this covered."

Seth picked up the cockroach, squished it between his fingers, and tossed it into the sink. Grinning, he flicked on the garbage disposal to grind the roach into mush, and then washed it down the drain. "Here," he said, reaching toward the girl, "give me your phone."

Reluctantly, Joan handed it to him. "Speak gently. My friend is really stressed."

He spoke very politely, and yet rudely. "Mia, my dear. Please prepare yourself to hear something of the highest order. Are you able to focus your intellect on something beyond your silly emotions?"

"*Excuse* me?"

"Mia Kittinger, you seem to have strong opinions about the nature of reality, especially regarding the sub-category of sanity."

"Um, can you give the phone back to Joan?"

"Listen, your friend is in mortal danger."

"Let me speak to her."

"I am not talking about Miss Dior."

"Then who are you talking about?"

"Ricardo."

Mia's heart pounded. "How is Rico in mortal danger?"

"I'm sorry to inform you about reality, but Ricardo had a relationship with Donna Murskey."

Eyes filling with tears, the girl replied, "I know, okay? I know."

"You need to know more. After observing you and Ricardo in the coffee shop, and having analyzed some of your online communications—"

"What!"

"Listen, Miss Kittinger. And I know Miss Dior will agree with me when I say this."

Joan scoffed, "I doubt if I'll agree with anything you say."

Seth glanced out the window at a sculpture of a dragon near the sinkhole. "Stay away from Ricardo. Don't meet up with him, don't call him, and don't even look at his texts. Delete everything about him. Understand? If you continue having contact with our little soldier boy, all hell will break loose."

Chapter 50

Deep in the Everglades, nuclear missiles were positioned in a secret military base to help with Armageddon. The strongest, bravest, most intelligent men were stationed at the base, but even the best soldiers of 1963 were completely unprepared for the Kingdom of Florida. The men were so ravaged by mosquitoes, their bodies became maps of indecipherable scars and they had to spray great clouds of poison into the air, killing a billion mosquitoes, and yet there were a trillion more. The tropical wings were relentless, intent on stealing every drop of blood while singing their swarming song of torture.

The Cold War sweltered in the Glades, with alligators circling in the steaming waters, and torrid panthers roaring at the melting moon, awakening soldiers from sweaty dreams (on the rare occasions when they slept). More than a hundred men were stationed in the mire. Horseflies like flying scorpions stung their faces, causing curses to rise above the cutting sawgrass while snakes rattled and hissed, spiders spun their webs, and the soldiers lived in a delirious fear of stingers, fangs, and venom. Heat lightning flashed as if exploding above the base, amplified by shrieking birds. An infinity of creeping things contributed to the suffering of the soldiers trapped in the heat, and yet they were willing to die for God and country, even in the torturous depths of the Kingdom of Florida.

Thankfully, the rockets were not launched, and nuclear winter did not descend. Armageddon was on its own calendar, unknown to the schedules of men.

Sworn to secrecy, the survivors of the base went on to other duties, some in the military and some in civilian life, all of them haunted by their time in the primeval. The base was abandoned to the snakes, spiders, alligators, panthers, and all creeping things.

And then, after nearly rotting away, the site was purchased by private investors.

In 1999, when amateur prophets were predicting the End of Days, the base was taken over by the WINGS. They restored many of the buildings, including the barracks, control room, and missile barns. The WINGS brought in mercenaries and more rockets, without nukes but with other incendiary powers, not to battle communists but to guard what they'd eventually plant, a seed from the Tree of the Knowledge of Good and Evil.

Chapter 51

"Our struggle is more spiritual than physical," the bishop said, sitting across from the reporter, "and we must remember that we share the universe with a diversity of created beings, including some that are malevolent."

Lil laughed. "Are you talking about aliens from other planets? Have you converted to Scientology?"

The bishop smiled and spoke as gently as possible. "This is basic theology, Lillian. Angels and demons. Special agents of Heaven and Hell."

She rolled her eyes. "Yadda, yadda, yadda. While you go hunting witches and warlocks, the corporations continue to dominate and possess the world. I'm not afraid of any witches, Bish. And I'm not afraid of ghosts. And I'm especially not afraid of angels or demons, because those things don't exist. Poof! A person grows up and doesn't need make-believe."

"Lillian, the existence of angels and demons has been revealed to us in manifest ways, such as, such as—"

"Spit it out, Bish."

He eyed the painting of the archangel. "I think we should go our separate ways, Lil, until tomorrow's Spiritual Warfare meeting."

"Warfare? You mean more cookies and coffee and repetitive prayers? Are you battling against super-powerful demons or the Knitting Ladies Club?"

The bishop winced and looked out the window. Diffused, horizontal light streamed through the blinds. "I know against whom we're battling, so our words must be tried and true, relying on the most potent phrases."

"Yadda yadda yadda. It's the same old, Bish. The same old."

"Like the sunrise."

The reporter sighed. "Here we go again."

"Yes. An ancient prayer is like a sunrise. The morning light may seem like the same old, when in fact it's a wildly different fire. Our prayers may seem repetitive and perhaps boring, but they're always a new dynamic of energy."

"Blah, blah, blah, sunrise. Is that all you have?"

There was much more that the bishop wanted to say to the struggling reporter, including his thoughts about how Mother Heron was helping them from above, and how the feebleness of the committee might make their spiritual efforts even more efficacious for the actual kingdom. They might even be saving some lives. But the bishop knew there is often no point in trying to overly explain the paradoxes of faith. So he just let it drop for the moment.

Chapter 52

The man from British Petroleum lay dead on the beach, having plummeted from the roof of the Breakers Hotel. The tide was rising as if to wash away the gray suit stained with blood and oil—and so the Palm Beach cops had the body surrounded in a half circle, shielding the view from various tourists and hotel employees.

"The medical examiner will be here soon," the captain said. "And keep an eye out for Beauchamp."

"Beauchamp?" a young sergeant said. "I wouldn't let that lunatic see this."

"He's already involved," the captain said.

The word *involved* was emphasized and the sergeant wondered if there was a double meaning in that. He wanted to ask more questions, but the medical examiner came bustling down the beach, her pale skin shining.

"Get away from my body!" she said. "Don't touch anything. You guys are always touching things."

Most cops avoided the woman from Iceland called "Florida Ice," but the captain gave her a warm smile. "A suicide," he said. "No signs of foul play."

The examiner, in a cold-blue pantsuit, spoke tersely. "You've been wrong before."

"Well, I'm right about this. And I'm sure Beauchamp will agree with my analysis."

"Perhaps," Florida Ice said, leaning over the body. "So much blood."

The captain nodded. "Yep. Getting impaled on a beach umbrella will cause some gushing."

"Hmm."

"What?"

"Look at his jacket—above the heart."

"Right," the cop said. "It's a mess."

"More than a mess. It appears to be a message."

"I don't see it," the captain said, wiping the sweat from his brow.

Ice gave the cop a glare that nearly froze his soul. "Are you blind? Look at the oil stain on top of the blood stain. It's a clear message." Slowly, the examiner traced above the smeary scribble. "*Rev 6.6.*"

"Dang," the captain said, squinting and leaning closer to the body. "There it is. *Rev six-six.* So. You think he was a reverend? We thought he worked for British Petroleum. The hotel manager said the guy was unbalanced. That was the word. Unbalanced. So maybe the guy believed he was a minister. Maybe he thought he was the Prime Minister. With all the crap happening in England, he needed to jump from the roof."

Ice gave the cop another chilling glare, blue eyes flashing. "Don't be stupid, Rick." She stood and walked over to the shade of a large, yellow beach cabana and called someone on her phone. "Hey. Where are you?"

"I'm in the woods. I'm almost out."

"You're in the woods? I have trouble picturing that. What if you get tree sap on your pretty white raincoat?"

"How did you know I was wearing my raincoat?"

"Because you know it's going to rain," Ice said, her voice wavering slightly. "The forecast says mostly cloudy skies, but you know it's more than that. And there's a hint of smoke in the air. Anyway, we've got a body at the Breakers."

Beauchamp had just been searching the crime scene where Mother Heron had been shot. "Another body?"

"Yeah, the Palm Beach cops are convinced it's a suicide, but I'm not sure."

Ee-yah! Ee-yah!

"Beauchamp, what's that awful noise?"

"Peacocks. They've been following me alongside the river. This place is swarming with peacocks."

"That's strange."

"Yes, the wilderness is full of eyes. And wings."

"Well, the deceased had no wings. He plummeted from the roof and hit an umbrella pole. The body is impaled."

"Fantastic."

Ice paused. "You're happy he got impaled?"

"No, I just made it out of the woods at the exact place where my car is parked. My black Charger is gleaming in the sun."

"Listen, Beauchamp. The body of the deceased is marked."

"Marked?"

"Yes. There's a message written in oil on his bloody jacket."

Detective Beauchamp could sense his girlfriend's nervousness. "Tell me the message."

"It's from the Book of Revelation," she said. "Revelation six-six."

"Oh," the detective said. "That's a bad one. I mean, nothing in the Good Book can be bad. However, that verse . . ."

Ice's voice trembled. "How bad is it?"

Beauchamp took a deep breath. "As bad as it gets."

Chapter 53

Dontey was called "the Beast" of the football field. The term was offensive in many ways, but he transformed the disrespect into an energy that fueled him to achieve more excellence. The football star was appropriately confident and truly humble, and if any of his friends needed help, Dontey was their best man.

"Joan, I got your text," he called out, climbing the stairs of the coffin-like building. "Joan? Are you here? Are you all right?" He reached the top and peeked through the window.

She tried not to shout, but sort of did. "I'm here!"

Rushing into the apartment, Dontey acknowledged the girl and said to the guy, "Don't you touch her. Don't you dare touch her."

"Greetings and salutations," the guy in the green suit said, stepping forward and extending his hand. "I'm pleased to meet you, Beast. I've seen you around, but we've never been properly introduced. I'm Seth."

Dontey glared. "The pleasure is all yours."

Seth smiled. "Would the Beast like some bottled water? Or perhaps a cola?"

It was a moment begging for a punch in the face and a punch to the gut. Dontey had every right to teach the guy a lesson in respect. However, because the legal system was known to put the wrong person in prison, Dontey chose to refrain from kicking Seth's butt, and instead spoke to Joan. "Did he touch you?"

"I'm fine."

Seth ran a hand through his thick hair as if searching for something like wisdom, or perhaps malice. "Actually, Dontey, you might be the one in trouble."

"Me?"

"Yes. You."

Dontey's eyes narrowed. "I doubt if you could —"

"Kill you?" Seth asked.

Joan snapped. "What? Did you really just say that?"

"Yes, I really said that. Your guy friend invaded my castle. And according to the law of this realm, I have the right to shoot him dead."

Adrenaline blazing, Dontey said, "Where I'm from, you don't threaten people unless you can back it up." He took a strong step forward, ready to hit the guy so hard that his raven hair would go flying.

"Okay, that's enough," Joan said. "C'mon, chill out. I want to ask Seth a few questions about Donna. And then we'll be gone."

"And then you'll be gone," Seth said, grinning. He sauntered over to the hallway closet and reached for the door handle. "Hey, Beast. Do you like to gamble? Care to wager whether or not I have a rifle in here?"

This would be an appropriate time, Joan thought, *for an angel to appear. Or a helpful giant.* But she didn't pause to see if they would make an appearance. Joan strode over to the closet and positioned herself between Seth and Dontey. "Don't start a war with us," she said.

Seth knew her spiritual strength came from a powerful source, but he'd been paid by the WINGS, handsomely, to start wars with many people. He chuckled at the teens in a way that sounded like his mouth was crunching bones, and he said, "Back off, you stupid, ugly witch."

It was the second worst thing that Joan had ever heard in her life, and she felt instantly numb, unable to reply or move or breathe. She merely stood there, face to face with the most handsome, horrific, dangerous person she ever hoped to meet, while the words echoed in her soul . . . *stupid, ugly witch.*

"Dude," Dontey said, raising his fists. He was angrier about the insult to Joan than he was about the threat with the rifle. "Did you really just say that? Did you really just beg to be slaughtered?"

Chapter 54

Down in the abyss on Apocalypse Island, the Ninth One grinned behind a skeleton mask. "There is no limit to what we shall do with human flesh. Already, we are past the embryonic stage of human consumption." He paused as if waiting for the red phone to ring, and then nodded at Agriculture. "Are we not just a few laws away from the entire food supply?"

Bone-thin and bald, Agriculture munched GMO wontons, took a sip of GMO soda, and began talking with his mouth full, drooling transmogrified drool. "Yes. Even the Salatin farm will be ours by Halloween."

Chapter 55

Joan and her mom were eating dinner on the sofa while watching the nightly news. The usual Florida stories splashed across the TV, including a pirate fiasco in Key West and a mermaid riot in Miami, but the mother and daughter weren't bothered by those stories while enjoying their pizza and iced tea.

Joan was relieved that the TV wasn't talking about the incident at the Gateway Garden in which two teens went flying out the window of an upstairs apartment—glass fluttering like crystal wings—and almost fell into the arms of a French giant, except he suddenly disappeared, and so the teens had to land on a huge pile of mulch while an unhandsome guy with a black eye and a broken tooth and a busted rib aimed his rifle and barely refrained from shooting because his phone began to ring—with a hiss.

"Good job making the tea, Joan. This is delicious, perfect amount of lemon. Cheers."

"Cheers, Mom," and they clinked their glasses.

Family, even when only two are gathered, still resonates with the original harmony of Eden, and so the discordant stories on the TV could not prevent the Diors from simply enjoying their lives together.

"Joan, I'll split the last slice of pizza with you."

"Heck yeah you'll split it with me."

Mom and daughter laughed and broke the crusty bread.

"Yum."

"That's what I'm saying," Joan said. "Yum."

"DRAGONS HAVE INVADED FLORIDA! This is a story you'll only see on Channel Six. Take a look at this unedited footage shot by a ranger in Everglades National Park, in which a Komodo dragon devours a deer. Komodo dragons are new to the park, although one of its relatives, the Nile monitor lizard, is already established in the area. Giant, carnivorous lizards are now in our neighborhoods, and

126

we ask our TV audience to be vigilant. Send us your footage of backyard dragons. And now we return to the IMMINENT THREAT OF WILDFIRES!"

A feeling of horror slithered up and down Joan's spine. The Komodo dragon was perhaps her least favorite animal in the world, known to dig up human graves and consume the corpses.

"I can't wait to go to Savannah," the girl said. "I wish college began tomorrow."

Her mom clicked off the TV. "That dragon didn't look real. It was probably a hoax, sweetheart. Don't worry about it."

"I'm not worrying. I'm just sort of . . ."

"What?"

"I don't know. Just sort of . . ."

"What? Tell me."

"Freaking out."

Leaning close to her only child, the nurse spoke with a voice that was both concerned and clinical. "When you say freaking out, does that mean sad? Or more like depressed? If I were to offer a diagnosis, honey, I'd say you're in mourning."

"In mourning? Yeah, I suppose."

"For that girl you found. An experience like that is extremely painful."

Joan paused before responding, wondering: *Should I mention Seth? And the rifle? And everything else?*

"Sweetheart, along with being in mourning for the Murskey girl, I know you're still grieving for your father."

Staring at her glass of sweet tea, Joan noticed that the droplets of humidity were flowing down like tears . . . or more like blood.

Chapter 56

Mia, after seeing the news on TV, went online to read everything she could about Komodo dragons, and then called Joan at midnight. "Listen to this! Komodo dragons dig up dead people! Did you know this? The residents on Komodo Island find the largest boulders available and roll them on top of graves to prevent the raiding of corpses. Can you imagine? Grave-robbing dragons! And the monsters attack living people as well. Joan, are you listening?"

"Do I have to?"

"Yeah, it's absolutely horrible. Komodo dragons have a condition like perpetual gingivitis. Their saliva is bloody. And poisonous. And venomous. One bite, and you become a zombie. I'm telling you, the dragons are the worst things on earth. And now they're in Florida."

"Way out in the Everglades," Joan said. "The dragons are far away from our houses."

"Far away from our houses? The Everglades are in our backyard. And it's the mating ground of all mating grounds. You know the python story. A couple giant snakes got tangled up near Homestead and suddenly thousands are slithering around. The same thing could happen with the dragons."

"Calm down, Mia. Just calm down. No dragon will appear in your yard and kill you. Okay? We live in town. Our moms pay taxes to keep the reptiles in the wilderness. We won't get attacked by a dragon."

Mia sensed a rising fear in her friend's voice and realized it wasn't wise to call at midnight when all sorts of things were slithering around Florida houses, and who knows what eyes were peering through Joan's window at that very moment.

"I'm sorry, Joan. I forgot how much you hate snakes and gators and all the creepy things. I don't like them, either. I just got carried away by the Komodo story."

"No worries," Joan said, her voice full of worry. "The dragon is out in the Everglades. And we're not going there. No way in hell."

Changing the subject, Mia said, "Joan, have you seen how you're blowing up the Internet? Really, you are seriously trending."

Because of one little tweet, thousands and thousands of people across the world had heard about Joan and her vow to track down Donna's killer. And not only that, someone had made a web page, showing Joan to be some sort of superhero. As if she didn't already have enough pressure to succeed.

Chapter 57

A server named Armando, his shift over at the café, sat in a booth beside the reporter and read the story on her laptop. When he was finished reading, he paused and then said, "Lil, you're suggesting that the padre murdered Donna."

"Yes. I think it was Father Adam."

"But you don't give any evidence."

Lil's hands trembled. She'd had four sugary coffees, and she'd been caught creating a scenario instead of proving the truth. She rasped, "Several witnesses said—"

"You don't name any witnesses," Armando objected. He was not a lawyer, but he once acted as a lawyer in a Cuban TV commercial. "I think you should name your witnesses."

"I don't have to! Anyway, the witnesses saw the priest at the scene of the crime."

"The day of the murder?"

"No, but on several other occasions."

Armando was not a religious person, but his mother and grandmother were, so he felt the need to defend the padre. "Here's what we know for sure. The retired exorcist visited Apocalypse Island at least twice. You have a receipt showing that he toured the Kennedy Bunker. And there's a photo of him smoking near the lagoon. But that was a month before Donna was killed."

"He was checking out the place. That's what ritual murderers do. They prepare for murder."

Armando shook his head. "You say Donna was killed on Apocalypse Island. But you don't know for sure. Maybe she floated over from Palm Beach."

"Or maybe aliens dumped her from a UFO," the reporter sniped. "Or maybe Skunk Ape stabbed her outside of a Lauderdale fishing camp and drove her body in an airboat to the lagoon. Yes, let's blame Skunk Ape for all earthly crimes."

Armando took a sip of Corona. He reflected for a while and took another sip. "Lil, your story doesn't make any sense."

The reporter's hands shook as if she'd lost control of them. "My story makes perfect sense! And I don't have to prove anything. I'm not a prosecutor. I'm just a giver of facts."

"You're not giving facts," Armando replied. "You're creating a story that might be fiction. And worse than that, you might be falsely accusing someone."

"Cranky Pants is guilty as sin," Lil muttered. She'd expected the server to praise her work, not challenge it. "Listen," she said. "If the priest is evil, and if he murdered the Murskey girl, then I want him to suffer for it."

Armando nodded and swigged his Corona. He thought back to their high school days at Cardinal Newman, and how Lillian was always a spitfire, challenging the teachers and administration about everything, suspecting conspiracies under every desk. She was so beautiful, in a thin, nervous way, but something in her soul was always dark, always accusing other souls of being dark.

"Lillian, my friend."

"Oh, shut up!" The reporter's eyes were all fire, darting from paragraph to paragraph.

"Can't you see? I've tied everything together. It's a cut-and-dried case. The exorcist became possessed, and instead of helping the girl in his care, he abused her. And then he murdered her!"

A cleaning lady named Renata, spiffing everything up in the back of the café, glanced over at the booth. She didn't speak much English but she understood the word *murdered*, which caused her to bow her head and make the sign of the Cross.

Armando whispered, "Lil, you need to revise the story. Why not make it more about good, and less about evil?"

"I want more *café con leche*! And a cigarette. Can I smoke in here, or will the cleaning lady kill me?"

Armando took a big gulp of Corona and wondered if Lil was on the edge of a breakdown. There were more things he wanted to critique in her story, but the reporter wasn't capable of feedback at the moment. Her eyes were wild and unblinking, and she glanced around like someone being hunted.

"I'd rather go to hell than change my story! It's *my* story! Understand?"

The cleaning lady stepped forward and aimed a bottle of disinfectant. "*Diablo loco.*"

"What? I'm not the *Diablo loco,*" the reporter replied, rising up. She grabbed her laptop and stomped away from the booth. "I'm a soothsayer! Do you understand? A sayer of sooth!"

Renata winced at the words. She did not understand them all, but she got the context. And when the café door slammed shut, the old woman strode forward and sprayed disinfectant where Lil had been sitting. "*Diablo loco,*" she repeated.

Chapter 58

Cheek-to-cheek, Beauchamp and Florida Ice graced the blue floor of the Mermusic Club. They danced like a couple celebrating a wedding (a topic currently off limits) and danced as if the world were young and the music of the first waters still flowed upon an earth that was always meant to be Eden.

The place was a dive. And all eyes were upon them while the band played swamp music.

Ice spoke with a melting voice. "Frederick, do you remember our first dance? It was right here."

"Of course I remember. Back when this place was called the Sunny Frog."

Ice smiled. "Sunny Frog? I don't think so. I'm pretty sure it was called the Cloudy Toad."

"Really? Are you sure?"

"Yes, my love. This place was never the Sunny Frog."

The lead singer of the band was covered with green tattoos and croaked about the cruelty of romance while the rest of the band grimaced.

"I like this song," Ice said. "It makes me feel like a teen."

Beauchamp laughed. "How awful."

"Yes, and glorious."

The detective gave her a little kiss.

"Eeewww!" The song groaned on like pure agony. "Eeewww, yeah, that's love!"

Whispering in the detective's dancing ear, Ice said, "Have you cleared the kid yet?"

"The kid?"

"Ricardo Vasquez."

Beauchamp nodded. "Rico is no longer a suspect. He never really was. Although . . ."

"Although what?"

The song ended. The lead singer tried to smile, couldn't do it, and croaked into the microphone, "That's all we got. Yeah. Whatever."

Frederick dipped Ice over the blue floor while a younger couple raised their drinks and whooped.

Returning to their table in the corner, Beauchamp and Ice continued their conversation. The detective spoke quietly. "The WINGS are still trying to frame Rico for Donna's murder. I encouraged that theory for a while—to keep their attention from the real investigation—but that game is over. I'm completely convinced that Donna was touched by the WINGS."

Ice sipped her water and licked her pale lips. "But the man from British Petroleum was not touched by them. There were no signs of a struggle. The *Revelation* thing on his jacket and the fall from the building—he did it all himself."

"Hmm."

Ice stared into the detective's eyes. "You don't agree with my findings? You think the guy was touched by the WINGS?"

"No. And yes."

"No and yes?"

"Exactly," Beauchamp said. "A paradox."

Shaking her head, Ice proclaimed, "There are no paradoxes for a medical examiner. It's either dead or alive. Accident or murder."

Two green-faced men at the next table overheard, and one of them croaked, "I'm a dead accident."

"I'm an alive murder," the other croaked.

"This is the sad truth," Beauchamp whispered to Ice. He rubbed his thin bluish line of a moustache, and his words were barely audible. "We struggle not with flesh and blood, but with powers and principalities."

Ice wasn't sure what he meant. "You think the government was involved?"

"No, not consciously."

"Subconsciously?"

Beauchamp paused. "I think most of human history has taken place subconsciously. Thoughts are the main way that evil influences the world. And nothing is more dangerous than a thoughtful, evil genius."

Ice sipped her water and half smiled. "Frederick, some say you're an evil genius."

"Well, they're wrong. Wrong on both counts."

"I think they're right. About one of the counts."

Beauchamp pretended to be hurt and raised his voice. "You think I'm evil?"

The toad-men let out several guffaws, and Ice gave them a cold look, causing them to retreat into some glowing, dark realm in their phones.

Ice whispered in the detective's ear. "You're a good genius. I'll listen to your theory. Will you tell me straight out, or subconsciously?"

"Straight out," he said, loud enough for everyone to hear. "The future will be profitable, insanely profitable, for people most knowledgeable in the ways of evil. Their bank accounts will swell like the bellies of the starving. The sellers of bread will live in gold fortresses, while billions of people will be slaves. Worker slaves. Sex slaves. Transhuman slaves. Whatever the bread sellers want to do with human flesh, they will do."

"Sounds good to me," a toad croaked.

"Me, too," another croaked. "Sign me up for the Antichrist."

"Idiots," Ice said, turning to face them. "Even if Armageddon never happens, you're still idiots."

"Takes one to know one."

Instead of threatening to shoot them, which Beauchamp might have done when he was younger, he merely ignored them. The detective stood like a star in an old movie and took his lovely lady's hand. "Shall we?"

"Dance? Until the End of the World?"

"No, my love, just until the music starts."

Chapter 59

"In the Everglades? Mia, are you insane?"

Mia stood like a safari princess in matching khaki pants, shirt, and bonnet. She posed outside the door of Joan's house and said, "It's cosmically inevitable. All of the forces of the universe are compelling us to visit the Everglades."

Joan glared through the screen door. "We're not going to the Glades. Understand?"

Continuing with her speech, Mia said, "Listen. I had a dream last night in which we were tromping through a snowy forest—"

"Oh, here we go again. I know this story."

"As I was saying, we were tromping through a mystical forest with shiny icicles decorating the trees like frozen teardrops of angels, and the sky was sparkling with huge snowflakes that flew around like heavenly doves, and—"

"I hate your recurring dream about how you become the Snow Princess and I get eaten by wolves."

"Listen," Mia said, adjusting her swamp bonnet. "In the middle of the frozen forest, in a vast clearing—"

"I know," Joan said, "I get devoured by wolves."

"No. There's a tropical garden in the clearing, full of—"

"Tropical wolves."

"No, let me finish. The garden is full of colorful flowers and artsy shrubs, and several rivers that meet up to form a beautiful lake, and palm trees, and—"

Joan's mother called out, "Let Mia in the house and shut the door. You're wasting air conditioning."

Instead of inviting Mia in, Joan decided to go outside and yell at lizards. "Shoo! Get out of here!" She stamped her boots on the cement to inspire a dozen newborn lizards, who were innocently sunning themselves on the sidewalk, to scatter into the bushes. "I'm not going to the Everglades, Mia. Understand? I need to stay in my room and do some computer stuff."

Mia sighed and whined (sort of like a Snow Princess). "Since you've become world-famous on the Internet, Joan, I suppose you'll be livestreaming updates for your supporters."

"Supporters? Have you seen the latest comments on Twitter? People are starting to turn against me, saying I'm a closed-minded little girl who doesn't know how the real world works, and that I should be sued for defaming upstanding members of society."

A few lizards crawled back from the bushes, claiming the edge of the sidewalk. Mia pretended not to see them, hoping her friend wouldn't notice the bulging eyes, scaly skin, and clawed feet. "Hey, Joan, I really think we should visit the Everglades."

Joan noticed the lizards. "You're out of your mind, girlfriend. I'm gonna lock myself in my room."

It would take Mia's greatest speech ever to inspire Joan to change her mind. The speech would need a perfection of rhetorical logic combined with guilt and temptation.

"Listen, Joan. You begged me to help you discover what happened to Donna. And here I am, your faithful friend, sharing my dream about overcoming Tropical Death—"

"You said the dream was full of flowers and artsy shrubs and—"

"Milkshakes," Mia said. "The best milkshakes in the universe are in the Everglades. Did you know that?"

"Best milkshakes in the universe? In the swamp? Doubtful."

"No, for real." Mia pulled out her phone and clicked on the website. "Here it is. An old-fashioned tourist trap called Robert is Here. Look. They have every fruit under the sun, and they make shakes out of everything. Guava, avocado, mango, papaya, coconut, key lime—"

"Mmm," Joan said, looking closer. "A key lime milkshake sounds good."

"Good? Try heavenly. And they have miracle fruit, too."

"Miracle fruit? What does that taste like?"

Mia grinned. "Miracle fruit tastes like fish, and chicken."

"Gross."

"C'mon, the whole place is a yum paradise. We can sample some fruit, have a key lime milkshake, and then maybe—"

"No," Joan said, eyeing the multitude of reptiles in her yard. "No way."

"Oh, c'mon. We'll have fun. You can bring your camera, and you can photograph the new life that sprang up after the last big storm. Isn't that what you artists do—share glimpses of new life?"

Stepping away from an overly curious lizard, Joan asked, "How close to the actual wilderness is the tourist trap?"

"It's between Homestead and Florida City."

"That sounds rural," Joan said. "That sounds like snakes all over the place."

"I doubt we'll see any snakes. You can even stay in the car. C'mon, Joan, I'll drive."

Two lizards met in the middle of the sidewalk and commenced battle, their scaly skin radiating an otherworldly glow. The scene made the tormented artist shiver, and she lurched toward the house. "I can't handle the Everglades, Mia. I'm sorry, but I have to say no. And I don't think you can handle them, either, not with that Komodo dragon skulking around."

"I've gotta follow my dream," Mia proclaimed, striding toward her shiny Fiat as if determined to go alone. And then, like she'd done in the finals of the national debate competition, Mia lowered her voice and delivered the devastating final line. "I'll just keep the secret map all to myself."

The words hung in the air like fruit from the most delicious and forbidden tree.

"Secret map?" Joan said, taking a step toward the battling lizards. "You have a secret map? For real?"

"Yes, *mon amie*. For real."

Chapter 60

The Spiritual Warfare Committee prayed the same old prayers in the bishop's office, "Our Father, who art in Heaven . . . ," while Lillian sat in silence, staring at a gaudy crucifix on the wall, tears streaming down her guilty face.

Chapter 61

The ocean groaned under the light of the moon and stars, and Donna Murskey, draped in black, strode up the beach. She climbed the dune of sand and seaweed, and paused for a moment when the baby kicked. Kicked, or was it a leap? Donna hadn't expected such movement to occur for another month.

The girl rubbed her belly and whispered, "Do you know something, baby? Are you trying to give me a message? Go to sleep now. Okay?"

Walking up to the ocean-side gate of the Ninth One's compound, Donna entered the code which she had stolen and memorized. The mechanical arm slowly lifted, and Donna snuck toward the garden. A foul smell filled the air, like rotten meat or a compost heap. Nausea overwhelmed the pregnant teen, and she felt faint. The thought entered her mind that she ought to go back home. Sneaking around the Ninth One's estate could get her killed. And anyway, why return the diamond necklace? It was her birthday present, so why not keep it, or sell it, or give it to the nuns?

A light flickered in one of the guest cottages. Donna hated that particular building. It was such a travesty of architecture, combining ancient Rome with an Aztec temple, decorated with steel swords and towering clay statues of snakes. A candle burned in the back bedroom, and wings fluttered over the roof, a frenzy of invisible things that Donna knew were always there, always watching. She bit her lip and continued forward while the candle spilled red light through the door and window as if to welcome her. She peered through the partially open door of the cottage, felt a surge of fury, and tossed the glittering necklace inside. "Take it back, you devil!"

Eyes wide in a flesh-colored mask, the Ninth One rose and approached her while the woman in his bed, Lil Reynolds, pulled a white sheet over herself.

"I take myself back," Donna said. "You had no right to have me. I was just a kid. Now I'm returning the last of your bribes, and I'm keeping my baby, and that's the end of it."

The necklace lay on the red-tile floor. "The end of it?" The Ninth One glared down at the large diamond, eyes flashing like black fire. "No, this is not the end of it." He lurched toward the wall and grabbed an antique sword. "Perhaps I shall cut the diamond down to atoms, and we can all share the wealth."

"I want none of your wealth," Donna said, turning away. "And I'm sick of your babble."

Wings whirred outside from the tops of palm trees, along with a loud croaking. The Ninth One stripped off his fleshy mask and took a shallow, wounded breath. "Donna Joy," he said. "Donna, my soul."

The words *my soul* sounded like an accusation while the pregnant girl ran away.

"Donna, return to the cottage! We need to talk."

"Let her go," Lil Reynolds rasped. She sank deeper into the bed and hoped she hadn't been recognized. "Please. Just let her go."

"Donna Joy, return to the magic," the Ninth One intoned in a charming voice. He wrapped himself in a towel and stuck his head out the door. "Bella Donna, Donna bella, return to your first love!"

"You are not my first love, nothing like it." The pregnant girl went to the edge of the ocean and waded into the water. The shimmering Atlantic was calm, the tide pausing between high and low, and there seemed to be an infinity of gentleness in the deep, and a promise that everything would be okay. The baby would be safe and happy.

The Ninth One marched like the ruler of the world toward the shoreline, calling out, "Bella Donna, what are you doing? Get out of the water!" While he marched through the sand, the ocean seemed to rise up to greet him. Or perhaps to stop him. Donna turned her back to the rising waves and stared at the man in the moonlight. She pointed and laughed at the supposed king who was wrapped in a white towel and wielding an old Roman sword.

"You. Are. Ridiculous."

"And you are," he said, nearly choking on his flattering reply, "the goddess of the deep."

The wind picked up, singing from the east and giving a stronger rhythm to the water, but the girl held her ground, waist-deep in the surf.

"I am not a goddess."

"Oh, but you are. And we have unfinished business."

Donna arched her back to keep her belly above water, and the thought crossed her mind to yell for help. She wanted to scream at the woman in the cottage to call 911, but she didn't think the woman would help.

"My soul." The towel-wrapped man stepped into the spindrift. "My pregnant soul, you are the IS. And the fruit of your womb will be a further sustenance."

The baby kicked, and Donna gestured toward the cottage. "If I'm your soul, then who is that in your bed?"

"A body," he replied. "Just another body that I need for my mission."

"Just another body?"

"Well, actually, she's a medium."

"Another one of your witches?"

"Something like that, but let not your heart go sinking. Look. The sky is soon to be light. Donna Joy, do you remember our helicopter ride? Do you remember when you told me you were pregnant? It was magic."

Donna did remember, of course, and kept silent. The wind was now wilder, waves rising and shoving her toward the beach, inching her closer to the sword.

"Oh yes, oh yes." The Ninth One aimed the sword at the girl's belly. "I recall very clearly how I carried you to the New Garden of Eden. I flew the helicopter myself, so that we could have a little secret. Was it not romantic, my love? Was it not a thrill to see the Tree?"

"No."

It was almost a suicide mission. The Ninth One did not respond to the orders from the missile base. He'd laughed when a voice commanded over the radio, "Identify yourself! Identify, or expect to be *fired upon!*"

"Obey the voice," Donna had said, rubbing her belly. "Or just turn around and get us out of the Everglades! I'm begging you."

Rockets were fixed on the copter while the self-proclaimed New Adam reached over to caress the teenager's thigh. In a dreamy voice, he sang, "Is this not a trip? We shall arrive and depart in a blaze of glory. Do not worry, we shall never die."

"Identify yourself! Or expect *fire!*"

"Please, please turn around," the girl pleaded.

"We shall be as gods," he sang, "and we shall never die. After all, I have deals with everyone. I own this Garden, and shall own it forever."

"Firing will commence in ten seconds! Identify!"

It would have been simple to stop the countdown. The soldier would have responded immediately upon hearing the voice of the Ninth One. But the New Adam was enjoying his game of immortality.

"Ten . . . nine . . ."

Donna screamed, "I'm carrying your child!"

". . . six . . . five . . ."

"And I'm keeping it!" Grabbing the controls, Donna caused the helicopter to circle the Tree as the voice on the radio said, ". . . two . . . one!" A missile flashed. Instantly the light was in their faces, death like a thousand strikes of lightning upon them, and yet the missile blazed away into the wilderness, just missing its target. The Ninth

One laughed and called down to the command center. "Code Eight-Eight-Nine. Abort."

"Yes, sir!"

"It is all meant to be," the Ninth One said, rubbing the girl's thigh. "We are above all the laws of the earth—in the magical flow of *IS*. We are the commanders of Paradise."

"I remember that brush with death," the girl said, struggling against the ocean while the waves pushed her toward shore.

The man pointed his sword and smirked. "There is a shark behind you."

Donna knew he was lying, but the thought of a shark hurting the baby was too much to bear. She wrapped her arms around herself to protect him.

"You are keeping my son from me," the Ninth One said. "He is the fruit of my spirit."

Those words almost made the girl faint. She took a few deep breaths to regain some strength, and then screamed, "He is not yours, and will not have your spirit!"

"The shark is still behind you," he said with a yawn. "I can see the dorsal fin. It's a great white. Hurry, come to shore. Take my hand."

The ocean swelled up while Donna staggered back. A shark could very well be near, swimming behind her at that moment. But a killer? No, the killer was on land, wrapped in a white towel as if he were innocence itself.

"Take my hand. Trust me."

Struggling to move backward against the swell, Donna shouted, "Throw the sword in the water! Throw it way out!"

"What? You know I paid good money for this magic blade. It once belonged to Caligula. Now come here. Take my hand, and deliver my son."

"No. He is not your son."

Angry tears streamed down her face, and Donna contemplated sinking beneath the surface, holding her breath and kicking toward home. She'd tell her parents everything—all of the secrets—and go with them to the police. It would be painful, but she'd accept that pain for her child. *Yes,* she thought. *I accept it.*

A huge wave crested and crashed against her. Donna raised her arms like wings, like an angel who could fly away, as she was thrust into the sword. "No! The baby!"

The Ninth One laughed, the sound nearly drowned by wind and otherworldly whirring while Donna fell and writhed in the sand. Lying on her back, everything darkening with blood, she could not see the tiny hand reaching out from the gash in her side. Certain that she was dying, Donna kicked at the laughing man and knocked away his weapon. "Don't you hurt him! Stay away from us!"

The Ninth One laughed and howled, and reached down toward her belly—his eyes full of emptiness—and ripped the child away.

"No! Don't take him!"

"Yes, my love. It is for the best." He picked up the sword and sliced the umbilical cord as if he'd done such a thing before.

Faint from loss of blood, Donna struggled to her feet. "Give me my son!"

"It is not yours. It belongs to those beyond you. It belongs to the deep."

"Give me my son!"

The Ninth One stuck the sword in the sand, and then began tickling the tiny chin of the boy like a proud father with real affection for his own flesh and blood. "What a sweet prince. Oh, what a shame." He tossed the bloody child as far as he could over the water, where the boy splashed down like a little fish.

Screaming, Donna surged into the surf and frantically swam out, blood foaming in her wake. The waves were rising and crashing all around, and Donna had no chance of finding the baby in that ocean. She believed she could hear a whimper on the wind, and she changed directions, again and again. Swimming and treading water and losing consciousness, Donna never gave up while she prayed, the words gurgling in her throat, "Mother . . . of . . ."

"Foolish nymph," the Ninth One said, shaking his head. He picked up his sword, rubbed it almost clean against his towel, and sauntered away to the cottage as if he'd just finished a typical walk on the beach.

A flurry of waves pushed Donna toward shore, but a riptide dragged her out to the deep. Blood spilled out of her body, and yet there was no pain, only a sensation of loss. Clinging to a hope that she and her child would find each other in the same current, the young mother sank over a cliff that descended into the abyss. Donna tried to breathe saltwater in a final attempt to locate her child. She did not choke. She did not breathe. Slowly, Donna Murskey sank into death.

She contemplated the cavernous deep, and it began to glow, and there were shadows—multitudes upon multitudes of shadows, including devil rays slow-flapping their wings as if they had eternity to waste down there.

Don't you hurt him!

That was Donna's only thought now: to save her baby. And all of the devil rays in the universe could not frighten her from her mission. Donna raised her arms above her head and dove, kicking her tired legs, descending into the watery cave and its multitude of shadows.

Go away!

The girl scattered the creatures, sending them down to where they could not be seen or cause any harm. And no matter how dead she already felt, Donna would not stop searching for her baby. She swam and kicked and gurgled more prayers, willing one thing: to save her son. The love of her life. The love of an otherwise wasted life.

Stephen.

The child, his skin shimmering as if the deep had sunlight that only shone on him, was not sinking, just drifting in a sort of equilibrium of grace. Donna prayed that she could live a minute more, and hold him in her arms and sing lullaby thoughts to him, and explain how life should have been, how life was meant to be from the beginning. However, there was no time left, except for the one remaining thing.

I baptize thee . . .

How beautiful was his flesh, the small perfection of his limbs resonating with the deiform soul. The world for him was all womb, and Donna's tears were as much from joy as from sorrow. She tried, but could not swim to where the boy was drifting, and so, with a final impulse, she raised her hand in a blessing.

The child looked up with adoring eyes, and just before his mother drowned, he gave her a wizened smile to show that he knew her only in blessing, and never in death.

Chapter 62

While Mia drove the champagne Fiat toward the Everglades, she glanced at her phone to see if Rico had sent more info about the map. There was no explanation, just the image.

"Keep your eyes on the road," Joan said, "you're crossing the line."

"No, I'm not."

The Fiat veered to the right shoulder of the interstate and almost hit a guy who was fixing a flat tire, except he was actually talking on his phone, pretending to fix a tire, and when he saw the Fiat he seemed quite animated, as if reporting information to someone.

"Keep your eyes on the road," Joan said. "Mia, if you cross the line one more time, I will literally leap out of the car. And I'll take the map with me."

One of the glorious things about having a Secret Map is that somebody gets to take possession of it, to keep it in a cave, vault, purse, pocket, or someplace where the precious parchment will be safe from the reach of others. Joan held the Secret Map in her artistic right hand while Mia swerved her Fiat through the manslaughtering Florida traffic. Staring at where X marked a spot, Joan said, "What do you think it means? It just says *Tree*."

"I don't know," Mia said. "But it might mean something about Donna."

"Rico never said a word about it?"

"Nothing. He just sent the link with no message. I texted him a bunch of times, but he won't reply."

Although Joan was edgy and brave, she was worried that the wilderness trip was beyond the scope of her mission. "I don't think we can figure this out," she said. "Not by ourselves."

"We don't have to solve everything," Mia said. "We'll just take a good look around. I have binoculars in my backpack. And if anything seems suspicious, we'll call the authorities."

"Authorities? You mean Beauchamp?" Joan had mixed feelings about the detective. "Can we trust him? He seems a bit creepy."

"I don't know if we can trust him," Mia replied, looking in the rearview mirror. "But I think he's following us."

And now, Dear Reader, somebody must die.

While the Fiat continued its treacherous journey among a mess of drivers who seemed to be driving for the first time, Beauchamp slowed the Charger and eased over to the far right lane, allowing the silver SUV with the flat tire (that wasn't really flat) to catch up.

The killer drove with his windows down, raven curls fluttering against his bruised face, while he flew toward the Charger that seemed to have stopped, or was perhaps backing up. Many cars are known to back up on I-95, so that was not surprising, but when the face of Beauchamp mocked him in the rearview mirror, Seth knew that this fight would take all of his murderous skills. It would be much more difficult than merely standing on a riverside and shooting a defenseless old Seminole woman.

Chapter 63

Rico stood near a payphone outside of a convenience store, getting pelted by a sun shower, waiting for a white-trash gangster to do some business. The guy holding the phone was shirtless, his skin a messy configuration of tats and pre-cancerous sun blotches. He whined, "It was my money to begin with! Man, like, dog, you know it was all mine! My dimes, and my nickels, too. What up, dog?"

"Excuse me," Rico said, losing his patience, "are you almost done?"

"Hold on, dog, you talkin' to me?"

"I have a situation," Rico said, hoping the gangster would empathize. "A situation with a female, and my phone's broke."

"You want me to stop holdin' the phone? Listen, dog, I had money that was mine to begin with, and now it's gone. My dimes, and my nickels, too. And a female. Like I don't know trouble. All right, dog? You good?"

"No, I'm not good. I need—"

The gangster turned away and continued his conversation. "Tell her what I'm sayin'. I want my dimes, and my nickels, too. What? No, that ain't right. Listen up."

Rico's blood was boiling in the hot rain. He wondered if he should keep waiting or go find another phone, perhaps in a better part of town. Shifting nervously, while the store owner stared out the window with recognition, Rico tried not to panic. He needed to stay very calm, even though someone had hacked into his phone and deleted Donna's messages, including the attachment of the map. He wished he hadn't sent it to Mia. What if the people that hacked his phone started monitoring her, too? Rico wanted to go to the police and tell them everything, but he was afraid they'd call him crazy, a conspiracy freak, or maybe even accuse him of murder again.

Murder again, he thought.

The sky rumbled with thunder, transforming the sun shower into something darker, something he'd never seen before.

Chapter 64

Spiral clouds like smoke whirled above Mia's Fiat while a storm began taking shape, rattling an obscene billboard that showed how far Florida had fallen from paradise.

DEAR READER, IMAGINE THE MOST VILE
AND HIDEOUS ADVERTISEMENT EVER.
OR, WAIT. DON'T DO THAT. IT'S TOO SICK
TO IMAGINE WHAT CAN BE SEEN IN FLORIDA.

A wind gust lifted a flock of crows from the billboard, a dark cloud flapping to the south like a many-winged monster.

This place is so weird, Joan thought. *It's wild and destroyed at the same time.*

Speaking of wild and destroyed, the man known as Seth, the WINGS assassin whose real name was Zorf, did not survive his high-speed crash with the low-speeding Charger, because Beauchamp was more in touch with reality and intuited the exact moment and location to allow the SUV to smack his bumper like a gladiating chariot. The detective swerved exactly nine degrees to the left and used metaphysical physics to spin out the killer, causing the SUV to skid off the road into a ditch, where it slid and came to rest in a sandy circle, a lovely oasis; and then *poof!* The SUV disappeared into a sinkhole, sinking quicker than quicksand and taking the assassin down to a hellish depth that no man—even if he had wings for hair— could ever survive.

Hello, Justice. Bye-bye, Zorf.

West of Fort Lauderdale, a green mountain arose near a condo wasteland, and Joan said, "Is that the highest hill in South Florida?"

Mia laughed sadly. "Yeah, it's a garbage heap, covered with sod."

"A mountain of trash beneath a layer of green," Joan said, glaring. "Talk about a cover-up. Talk about false appearances."

"Florida is very complex," Mia said, looking in her rearview mirror at a black vehicle that might have been a Charger or a hearse. "You remember my speech about the strange history of Florida."

Joan didn't answer, politely allowing a pause, knowing that her friend wanted to give the speech again.

"When Henry Flagler ruled the kingdom, Florida became less about reality and more about appearances. Colorful postcards with towering palm trees were sent around the world, beckoning people to a tropical paradise. However, the coconut trees were fake. Well, not fake, but they weren't native. They were imported for show, like the making of an epic movie about the Garden of Eden. Florida is less of a place and more of a scripted drama. Only the Everglades are real. At least they were real, before people messed them up. Did you know there used to be fewer snakes in the great river of grass? Because there were more bears and panthers. Now, with fewer snake-eaters, the slithering reptiles are everywhere."

"Mia?"

"Yeah?"

Joan felt a bit sick. "Can we go home now?"

Nudging her friend's shoulder, Mia said, "C'mon. The fun is about to start."

"I don't feel good."

Not answering, Mia accelerated toward the Everglades, hoping the delights of the fruit stand would bring healing to her best friend.

Joan stared sorrowfully out the window, her attention drawn to a festering sight of abandoned limestone quarries. The pools of green water seemed putrid, the color of liquidized reptile skin, making the artist more nauseous.

Mia glanced over with a sisterly smile. "Just a few more miles, Joan, and then we'll be enjoying the best milkshakes in the universe. And we'll get some laughs at the petting zoo. They have fainting goats. They go baaa! And then faint. Baaa! And then faint. It's awesome."

"Thanks. I'll pass."

"Fine, stay away from the cute goats. And stay away from the python, too. But you'll want to meet the miniature pony. Snowbird the pony. Totally awesome, right?"

Closing her eyes, Joan thought, *Just shoot me now.*

Chapter 65

In the Primitive Holy Ghost Apostles Church of Pentecost and Deliverance, the pews were empty on a weekday morning, but the pulpit was full of thunder. The minister wore a black suit with a red handkerchief in the breast pocket. His forehead sparkled with large beads of sweat, and he shouted, "Word has gotten out! We've heard it in the heights, and the powers of this world will fall from their places! And the meek are ready for rising, rising like a chorus to the heavens, rising to inherit the many mansions lost by vaulting ambition! Word has gotten out, echoing back to the beginning and singing again for a future where the last word will be love! And love will save the meek! And love will sting to death the Devil's angels!"

There was an echo in the back of the church. "Devil's angels . . ."

Squinting to see who was rising from the shadows, the minister was ready to confront the intruder. Crime was not uncommon in the Tamarind Avenue neighborhood. Only yesterday, he'd scared away some vandals.

A tall, young man walked down the center aisle, his every step a witness to strength. If he was looking to cause trouble, he could have inflicted a great deal. However, the muscular youth wasn't visiting the church to inflict harm, but rather to offer his father respect—in the form of asking for advice.

"Hey, Pops, sorry to interrupt," Dontey said, "but I need your opinion about something, if you're not too busy."

The minister wiped his brow, thinking about his sermon, wondering if he should make a stronger connection between Isaiah and Revelation.

"Pops, I hope you can help me with a dream I had last night. It was wild, and I don't know what it means, or if I should do anything about it. I hoped maybe you could—"

"Girl trouble?"

"Well, sort of. But she wasn't in the dream."

"Does she have a name?"

"Like I was saying, Pops—"

"No girls in your dreams. Good. That's for the best. You should be focusing all your dreams on college."

Dontey glanced at the songbooks piled near the pulpit, then focused again on his father. "There was a cathedral in the dream, Pops, like something from the Middle Ages. Near the altar, a knight battled a creature that was both a snake and a dragon. The knight hacked with an axe, but the creature wouldn't die. It seemed like they fought forever, and the knight was losing. And then I woke up. Don't know who won. What do you think it means?"

Wiping his brow again, the minister sighed. "You know what? Your mother is better at interpreting this stuff. It's not really my gift. Maybe you should tell her about the dream."

"She's already at work."

"Right. Well, you could call her."

Dontey shook his head. "It's all right. It's just a stupid dream, anyway. No rule says it has to mean something."

Leafing through his Bible on the gleaming pulpit, searching the last few pages, the minister said, "Where is that picture? I thought it was in here."

"What picture?"

"I can't find it. Huh. I could have sworn. Dang."

"Don't swear, Pops. And you probably shouldn't say 'dang' in church either."

Laughing, the father said, "You got that right. Word might get out."

"Right, well, I have things to do. And you better practice your sermon. Sounds like a good one."

"Yeah, I need more Isaiah connections to Revelation," the minister said. "These days, everyone needs more Isaiah with Revelation."

Dontey nodded respectfully and began turning away from the pulpit.

"Son, hold on. Let me tell you about the picture."

"What picture?"

"In the back of my Bible. There's a picture of Saint George and the Dragon."

"Saint George?"

"It's an English thing. From the King James Version, right?"

"Yeah, that's cool. I'm down with the thees and thous."

The minister smiled. "Let me ask thee a question."

"Okay, Pops. I'll try to give thee a good answer."

"Were you the knight in the dream? Or was it someone else?"

Dontey closed his eyes, trying to remember. "Yeah, I think I was the knight. It was weird, like I was watching myself have another life."

"Well, you should ask your mother for her interpretation—she's the expert—but I think I figured it out."

Dontey's eagerness for the answer made him feel as if lightning were about to surge through the building.

"Here's what the dream means," his father said. "Are you listening?"

"I'm always listening."

The famous minister nodded proudly, and then his face grew serious. "Are you ready for the message?"

"I'm ready."

There was a long pause, similar to other long pauses that have filled churches from the beginning, inspiring the silence that is also a tongue of angels. Hazy, rain-colored sunlight poured through the window.

"Pray."

"Pray?" Dontey asked. "That's it? What should I pray for?"

155

Shrugging, his father answered, "The same thing Adam prayed for. Think about it. The moment he stumbled out of Paradise and into the fallen world, he must have asked God to kill the Devil. Can you imagine how much Adam must have hated that serpent?"

"I'm sure he did want him dead and gone."

"Exactly."

"So," Dontey said, narrowing his eyes, "you think my dream means I'm supposed to kill Satan?"

The minister shook his head. "You're one of the greatest athletes in the history of Palm Beach County, and you'll be a superstar at Florida State. But you, Dontey, cannot kill Satan."

Dontey thought about the battle-axe and the blood gushing from the serpent, and he asked, "Can a person wound him? Can a person weaken him?"

"Just pray," the minister said, wiping his brow. "Be a spiritual athlete. And understand you're not the star. Let the angels chase down the Devil."

"Chase him down in Florida?"

"Everywhere in the world. And yeah, especially in Florida."

Chapter 66

Inside the famous tourist trap, Mia led a sickly Joan through colorful rows of exotic foods that made the fruit stand seem like a dream. "I'd love to own a fruit farm," Mia said. "Don't you think, Joan? A bountiful garden of Eden to enjoy and share the bounty with others? Hmm, maybe I won't become President of the United States. Maybe I'll just learn how to farm and live a simple life, spending my time in the sweetness of the orchards—"

"Lizard man!" Joan gasped.

"What?"

"Out the back window in the petting zoo—look."

Mia leaned around a tourist and craned her neck to see. "Lizard man? I just see goats—oops, one just fainted—and a pony. Are you messing with me?"

Blinking, not sure if she'd seen another vision, Joan tried to joke it away. "Too much transhumanism in the news, I guess."

"Well, technically, a lizard man would fall in the category of *chimera*. Rico and I watched a video about chimeras and Armageddon."

"Drop it, Mia."

"Hey, don't be so bossy. I was just helping differentiate scientific abominations. Anyway, isn't this place great?"

Joan sniffed the air—a hundred lovely scents mixed with the olfactory menaces of animal manure and wildfire smoke—and she sneezed.

The Secret Map went flying, floating in the air over crates of mangoes, and slowly fell at the feet of a man who resembled a goat. "What do we have here?" he gruffly asked. He stooped to pick up the map. "This looks interesting."

Mia lurched for the document and butted heads with the guy. Her safari-princess bonnet helped cushion the impact, yet she still yelled, "Ouch!"

While Mia stood dazed for a moment, Joan reached down and retrieved the map, hiding it in the back pocket of her skinny jeans.

"You better be careful," Goat Man said, rubbing his curly skull. "You better keep that map safe, or you'll see it on the Internet."

"It's none of your business," Mia said. "Now please excuse us." She took Joan's hand and woozily led her friend around a row of guava to the milkshake counter. "Let's get our sugar fix, and get the heck out of here. Look at the item board, and don't even think about a lowly smoothie."

"A real shake does sound good," Joan said. Her stomach felt better at the sight of a long list of concoctions. "I never knew so many milkshakes existed. Passion fruit. Star fruit. I guess you can put anything in a blender with ice cream and get something yummy."

A hot breath bit the girls' necks and Goat Man said, "I suggest the dragon fruit. And the monstera. Yes, the monstera ripened early."

Joan's skin crawled at the thought of eating anything that contained the word *dragon* or *monster*, and yet she seemed influenced by the suggestion. "One monstera milkshake for me, please, and one dragon for my friend."

"Yum," Mia said. "I sort of wanted key lime, but dragon's even better."

Nodding his approval, Goat Man turned from the girls and accosted a Japanese tourist. "You should try the Komodo shake. You should buy the extra-large."

The tourist responded reasonably well to a situation like that. "*Domo arigato, Goatzilla.*"

Mia's phone rang at that moment, and she ignored it. "It's probably Rico."

"Aren't you answering? You wanted him to call, right?"

"No," Mia said coldly. She reached down into the girly debris of her handbag, pulled out the phone, and checked for his name. "Huh. It's not Rico. It's an unknown number."

"Maybe you should answer."

"It's probably a telemarketer saying I won a fabulous cruise to the Bermuda Triangle."

"Answer it."

"I can't handle a salesman now."

Goat Man snuck up again, caressing the girls' necks with his foul breath. "The petting zoo is out back," he said. "You can make friends with cuddly, scary animals. Want to make friends with them?"

Already freaked out, Joan shoved some money at the cashier. "Hurry up with the milkshakes. Keep the change."

Laughing and snorting, Goatzilla trotted over to a whole group of Japanese tourists. "You people like weird animals, correct? *Deshioka?*"

A woman bowed and spoke with a whisper, which meant, very loosely translated, "Please leave us alone politely and die."

"Here are your milkshakes," the cashier said. "Enjoy. And if you're going into the Everglades, I wouldn't go far. There are wildfires on the western edge, and a storm is blowing in. Even with rain, the fires will get worse because of lightning. We're shutting down the market early today."

"Thanks for the warning," Mia said.

The girls took their elixirs to the parking lot, where the sky crackled with green lightning. "I'm sorry, Joan. We never should have driven out here. I think we should leave now. It's starting to look scary."

"It's actually quite beautiful," the artist replied. "And this milkshake. Wow. I love it."

"Really? You feel better?"

"I am feeling better, *mon amie.*"

Joan sipped while contemplating the swirling heavens, and then took out the map, unfolding the paper slowly. She studied the simple imagery of a military base, a strange light rising from the ground, and an island with a glowing tree. The map seemed to make a greater impression on her the more she looked at it, actually drawing her in with a vision, although blurry, of some unparalleled adventure and hieroglyphic path to heroism.

Looking up at the swaying palms, Joan said, "The wind isn't that bad. I think it's dying down, and it's not raining at the moment. The wildfires are way out west. What harm would there be in exploring an old military base? And maybe, if things seem okay, we can follow the map a little more. If it has something to do with Donna, then we have to risk it. At least I do. I have to risk everything for her."

Mia hesitated, took a sip of her shake, and then nodded. "Okay, but you'll need my Fiat."

"So that's a yes?"

"Yes, Joan. Let's crash that military base."

Chapter 67

"Rico? Is that you? Your voice is shaking."

"Listen, Dontey. Some bad stuff is going down. Are you at your house?"

"I'm at the church."

"Wait for me there, okay? I'm in the neighborhood. But if you see any strangers approaching, run for it, and I'll meet you at the salvage yard."

"What's up, Rico? The police tracking you? Beauchamp after you again?"

"Just wait for me. Okay? And don't call Mia or Joan. We need to see them in person. Something big is going down."

Chapter 68

The gray helicopter was the pinnacle of flying arts, faster than most airplanes and equipped with a sound system that blended the whirring blades with a seismic bass line, making every flight an underground rave in the sky.

The Ninth One believed himself to be Master of Pilots and King of the Atmosphere. And he wore a blue mask when he flew.

"Why do you wear that stupid thing? It makes me laugh."

The exotic girl in the passenger seat was from all around the world. Middle-Eastern born, she was purchased as a baby and became known to those who know the most of earthly matters. Nubile young, yet seemingly two thousand years old, the girl had risen in popularity after Donna's death.

On a whim that felt like cosmic fate, the Ninth One invited the new beauty to fly up to St. Augustine. "My goddess, shall we look down upon the ghosts?"

The girl raised a pierced eyebrow. "Look down upon ghosts?"

America's most ancient town was said to be haunted, and the gray helicopter hovered above like an angel of death. The Ninth One boomed his voice into the sound system. "The first Thanksgiving was celebrated in St. Augustine in 1565, threatening to make *La Florida* a realm of other wings, but now we own everything from coast to coast."

Yawning, the girl said, "Whatever. I want to see Magic Kingdom."

The helicopter whooshed through the sultry air, over pink houses built on swamp-sand, over palm trees imported from Morocco, and over the straight and serpentine roads that joined in the tangle of Orlando. There, hovering over turrets and spires, the girl was pleased. "We all dream of being royal," she said. "We all want to live in a magic castle."

"I own it," the Ninth One said.

"You own Disney?"

"Yes. My partners and I. We own as far as the third eye can see. We have deals with everyone. Did you notice Cape Canaveral when we flew up the coastline? We own that."

"The US government owns that."

"Exactly. My partners and I downsized the space program because the astronauts were getting too close to proving the existence of the highest power, and that would not be good for the terrestrial economy. For our purposes, we cannot allow the heavens to declare more glory."

"You're crazy," the girl said.

"Yes, crazy like a fox. Like Herod. And Caligula. Those guys had some tricks."

The girl grinned knowingly. "They had tricks. And weaknesses."

"Indeed. They did, and died, and are dead."

"But you have no weaknesses, only strengths."

The Ninth One nodded, admiring her flattery. "If you partake of another secret with me, you may rule a magic kingdom."

"Oh, no, thank you," she said, looking out the other window. "Ruling is too much effort. I don't want to rule the kingdom. I just want to own it."

"And serve the ruler?"

"And be served."

The Ninth One pointed to where thousands of commoners were gathered around the castle. The commoners gaped and gestured as if the helicopter were part of a glorious show, as if the Ninth One and his new Eve would leap out like fireworks incarnate.

"Look at the masses," he said with disdain. "Their hearts are burning for an ecstasy beyond imagination. And yet they remain on the ground."

"And we're up here," the girl said, "where we belong."

Willing the helicopter to rise higher, making the castle shrink to the size of a playhouse, the Ninth One gestured, sweeping his hand over the realm of Orlando. "Do you really want it? You can have it, if you really want it."

"Hmm," the girl said with a shrug. "What else have you got?"

The Ninth One stared at an image on the control panel. "Trouble," he said. "Some real trouble—that may lead to some excitement."

It was an image of Joan, trespassing.

Chapter 69

TRESPASSERS WILL BE SHOT.

"I think we're safe," Joan said, stepping up to the barbed wire. The old military base appeared to be abandoned, or if not completely abandoned, it didn't seem like a launching site for missiles but simply a research center.

Mia had the map now, her nose almost touching the parchment, her hair curling down from her bonnet like wisps of blonde flame. "Stay away from the fence, Joan. It might be electric. And we don't need to climb it. The Tree is about a mile in the other direction—straight into the wilderness."

The reality of walking into the River of Grass, with its snakes and spiders and alligators, made Joan's heart sink. Being heroic in theory was one thing, but walking into the actual Everglades was probably beyond her heroic capacity. She was more willing to risk whatever was inside of the research center. Joan grabbed the fence and gave it a little shake. "It's not electric," she said, holding tightly between barbs. "We can climb it, Mia. I think we should explore the buildings, gather information, and then go home before the rain gets nasty. And besides—"

"Besides what?"

"Take another look at the map. Look at this." She pointed at the fluttering page. "See the moat around the island? There's no way to get across that moat."

"Of course there's a way," Mia said. "There's always a way." She turned as if modeling her nice green backpack.

Joan paused. "What good is a backpack against a moat?"

"It's packed with helpful things."

"Like a catapult?"

"No, something better than a catapult."

"What's better than a catapult?"

165

Mia grinned, because she actually had a good answer for that. "Inflatable kayak. You just pull the cord, and it fills with air. And we'll sail across the moat. Easy peasy. So. Are we marching onward, or what?"

Shivering in the humidity, Joan stared at the vast Everglades, her eyes scanning the wild terrain for signs of natural and unnatural dangers, and then she took in the higher horizon, a swirling, primeval sky. She gulped a deep breath of smoky air, terrified yet emboldened to keep on following the map.

Chapter 70

In the sulfurous bowels of Apocalypse Island, an emergency meeting was called by Weapons to discuss "the problem of the Ninth One."

The WINGS, not waiting for Porn, who was delayed for some noxious reason, huddled in a semicircle around the red phone.

Weapons: "Our next move must be decisive."

Technology: "And invisible to the public."

Oil: "Yes. The action must be buried, with no chance of arising."

Banks: "Should the Ninth One be touched today? Or deferred?"

Media: "Why wait? We know he murdered the Murskey girl. There was a witness."

Oil: "And a leak. He was never careful with blood."

Banks: "He's more trouble than he's worth. He gives WINGS a bad name, and he would mortgage all of us to save himself."

Media: "Our image is wounded. But we can heal that. Just say the word, and there will be a legion of stories going viral."

Banks: "Yes, we can buy as many stories as we need, until there is only one story. But what is our reality at this moment?"

Weapons: "The Ninth One is in the air again. We'd agreed that nobody would fly until tomorrow morning when we'd descend upon the Tree together. We were to make no unilateral decisions, and now he's acting alone."

Media: "He is not alone. He has a new girl with him."

Weapons: "We were always worried about the possibility of the other families getting involved."

Banks: "She is not from an old family. Nor is she from a new family. I can verify that."

Oil: "The new girl seems to have arisen from no family."

Media: "Whoever she is, we'll touch her and bury her, along with the Ninth One."

Pharmaceuticals: "If we touch them today, will we visit the Tree in the morning? Are we keeping with the ritual and the eating of the fruit?"

Banks: "If the answer is yes, there is no going back. There is only the now and the *IS* and the enriching of the prophecy."

Agriculture: "Laborers will work ten days for a loaf of bread."

Banks: "We'll own the bread."

Technology: "We'll be presented as gods. The Eight Wings. We'll monitor every move and idea, and intervene as necessary."

Weapons: "Good, we have agreed. If the Ninth One returns to the airport, we'll detain him and the girl there. And dispose of them elsewhere."

All: "Yes."

Weapons: "And if his copter approaches the Tree, we'll shoot it down and allow nature to take its course."

All: "Yes."

Weapons: "And there won't be anything left of them. Not one speck of flesh. Not one drop of blood. Agreed?"

All: "Agreed."

Weapons: "Hell yeah! Now who wants to eat more Chinese?"

Chapter 71

"Sawgrass looks so harmless," Joan said, studying the tiny teeth.

"Don't touch it," Mia lectured. "Sawgrass has a design similar to a serrated knife. It can cut you terribly, and there's no doctor out here to stitch you up."

"I keep reaching for it, to keep my balance," Joan said. "I'm afraid I'll sink otherwise."

"You won't sink. Most of this area is pretty dry until the big rains come."

Joan nodded and took a more confident step, and another confident step, and suddenly sank. She flailed her arms as if trying to fly from the deadly depths. "Help! Help me!"

"Oh, you're fine," Mia said, trying not to laugh like a know-it-all. "You just stepped in a solution hole."

"Solution hole? Solution? I have a solution! Give me your hand and pull me out!"

Mia tugged and chided, "Look, your feet aren't even wet."

"That's weird. I was afraid I was sinking down to . . . down to . . ."

"Limestone. Most people don't realize the Everglades are mostly stone."

Dear Reader, did you know that? Isn't that fascinating? Don't you wish you were tromping over limestone death pits?

"Watch your step," Mia said. "Some of the solution holes are six feet deep."

Trying to avoid the subterranean traps, Joan walked warily and asked, "What happens to the solution holes during the wet season?"

"They fill with water."

"Only with water?"

"And wildlife."

"Wildlife," Joan echoed, her eyes darting in all directions. "You mean alligators."

"Yeah."

"Wildlife," Joan said, suddenly looking behind her back. "You mean pythons."

"Yeah."

"Maybe we should run to the island, and immediately run back, before the rains fill the solution holes with reptiles."

Mia looked to the sky. It was hazy, but not too stormy, some swirls of moisture mixed with wisps of smoke. "We're safe for the time being. No need to run, but let's keep on marching."

Marching and slapping at vampiric mosquitoes, the girls said, "Ouch." Sometimes individually and sometimes in harmony. "Ouch!"

Red dragonflies also buzzed around as if on secret patrol, and turkey buzzards circled above, searching for carrion while rattlesnakes coiled silently beneath the deep shade of palmetto trees. The explorers traversed sawgrass, ragweed, thistle, and creeper. They didn't speak much, trying to stay focused on the mission.

"Listen," Joan said, suddenly stopping. "Did you hear that?"

"I hear the wind," Mia answered, tightening her bonnet so it wouldn't blow away.

"That's all? You don't hear anything else?"

Mia stared at the island of swaying trees. "I hear music in the branches. And a bird calling."

"No. There's something else. Can't you hear it? Listen!"

"Listen to what? Why are you acting so strange?"

Joan seemed on the verge of a panic attack, but she closed her eyes and fought it, convincing herself that her fear was irrational, and that she hadn't really heard the heavy breathing of a dragon.

"Never mind," Joan said, opening her eyes. "Let's keep going. It's probably nothing."

"Hold on," Mia said, searching her friend's worried face. "Tell me. What did you hear?"

"It was just my imagination, so let's keep moving," she said, stomping forward. "Look at those clouds, circling around like the rings of Saturn."

Mia sniffed the air. "More like smoke. Can you smell the smoke?"

"No," Joan said. "I don't smell any smoke."

Sniffing, Mia tried to figure out if the wildfires were a hundred miles away, or fifty, or five. "I don't want to burn up," she said. "I'm not afraid of death, but I don't want to burn."

"We're not going to burn," Joan whispered under her breath.

"So you think we're safe?"

"Safe? We're in the freaking Everglades. No, we're not safe. Mia, stay alert."

Increasing their pace, the girls helter-skeltered through the grassy river, barely avoiding various pits and multiple creepy-crawly things with teeth, venom, and poison. Mia was doing most of the work, hefting the backpack, and she was eventually lagging behind, panting for breath. "I need to rest. Hey, slow down! I need to rest."

"Oh, okay, sorry," Joan said. "I should have offered to carry the pack. Here, I'll take it. But let's not stop for long. If we're going to discover anything on that island, we'd better get there soon."

Mia slipped the pack from her shoulders. "Just give me two minutes. Okay? And then we'll go fast. To the moat."

"To the moat," Joan echoed softly. She stared deeper into the wilderness and thought: *Now that we're this close, will I have the courage to cross over?* A blast of smoky wind caused her to turn and glance back at the road. And she saw, crawling toward where the Fiat was parked, a long black hearse.

Just my imagination, she thought. *Why drive a hearse out here?*

Chapter 72

The sniper stood near a poisonwood tree and aimed his rifle at Joan. His orders were to touch her with a bullet through the heart. He was one of five full-time assassins that formed a pentagon of protection around the Tree of the Knowledge of Good and Evil. However, because of wildfires, the other snipers had joined forces with the missile crew to help control the flames out west. Hostiles, like the two girls, were not usually a problem and were always caught before they'd gotten very close to the island. Snake hunters, gator hunters, bird watchers, students, tourists, or whatever lost soul happened to stumble near the new Eden would be released with just a warning.

The order of this day, however, was the sniper's favorite: shoot to kill.

Joan reached the moat and paused near an unseen rattlesnake. Waiting for Mia to catch up again, she gazed across the water and tried to discern what the map showed as the *Tree*, but the island was a jungle with no way to see the center. It was overgrown with ferns, strangler figs, palms, and poincianas with red blossoms dripping like thick drops of blood.

Red lightning reverberated in a lowering sky, and the sniper slowly squeezed the trigger. Joan's back was in the scope, an easy shot, except that her heart was protected by the backpack. So the sniper paused and repositioned himself. *A head shot would be easy enough*, he thought. He'd blazed bullets through heads before—in wind and dust and deserts across the world—for lesser masters. But the Ninth One, who owned them all, believed that a good assassin "must always touch the heart."

"Here," Mia said, approaching the moat, "I'm finally here. Let me help you inflate the kayak. This morning I memorized the owner's manual. Let me pull the cord thingy."

"Okay. It's all yours." Joan dropped the backpack on the grass, causing the rattlesnake to slither away as a crackling sizzle shot across the Everglades. Joan staggered and gasped, blasted by a gust of wind.

Mia warned, "Watch out. Florida is ground zero for lightning. Even though it rains more in the state of Washington, you're ten times more likely to be struck dead in Florida."

The sniper aimed again, waiting for Joan to stand still, waiting for her heart to align perfectly in his sights. He would touch her first, and then touch the other girl. He would wait for another round of thunder to cover his sound and make it seem like the heavens had fired the shot.

"Now."

A bullet burned through the air and found its target, splitting a rib and puncturing a lung—and yet missing the heart.

Watching the sniper fall, Beauchamp knew that his police pistol had made a good shot from very long range, and he also knew that the sniper was merely wounded, writhing beneath the poisonwood tree. The detective pulled himself out of a solution hole and began hunting his prey, ready to fire again.

Joan and Mia didn't hear anything but thunder, so they continued with their plan. The kayak inflated nice and plump, and Mia dragged it over to the moat, where it almost flew away, but she managed to plop it on the water. "C'mon, we don't have much time."

Joan stood by the shore, staring at her phone. Raindrops splattered the screen, blurring the dull light. "There's no signal."

"Yeah, I know. Climb in. It seems pretty safe. Pretty legit."

The wobbly kayak did not inspire Joan's faith. "I think we should go back home."

A shadow swirled and disappeared in the moat, unnoticed, while Mia tried to speak bravely. "There's no going back now. This is where Donna wants you to be. Can't you feel her presence? She wants the truth to be known. She wants you to fulfill the vow. Can't you hear Donna's voice in the wind?"

Joan listened, and all she could hear in the wind was doom, punctuated by lightning and thunder. And now it sounded like gunfire.

Chapter 73

The Spiritual Warfare Committee continued to pray while Lil Reynolds removed herself from the circle and slunk over to a side table near some bookcases. She sat at the table and found a pen and paper in a drawer. "Tell the truth," the reporter told herself. "Write nothing but the truth."

Lil took a deep breath and began writing a revision of her story.

Confession in Paradise

I witnessed the stabbing of Donna Murskey. I will be forthcoming with the details, including my failure to save Donna's life. But first I must say this about the young woman who was said to be a 'bad girl.' In the depths of reality, Donna Murskey was a beautiful soul.

Chapter 74

The sniper writhed beneath the poisonwood tree, gulping bloody breath, trying to regain the strength to kill. Smiling manically, he was pleased by the exchange of gunfire because that was what he lived for.

Beauchamp was sprawled in the grass, gritting his teeth, a bullet lodged in his right leg. He should have made a tourniquet of his raincoat to slow the flow of blood, but there was no time to think about saving his own life. Joan and Mia were doomed without his help. The detective raised himself from the wet ground and limped forward. He had little time before the sniper would also rise, rifle flashing with another round.

Don't let him see you. The landscape was more than hostile, jagged limestone intermixed with sawgrass, spike rushes, and rattlesnakes. Even if Beauchamp didn't take another bullet, he was perhaps as doomed as the girls. He fell into spike rushes that punctured his face. *Don't make a sound!* His eyes filled with red while the rain and smoke swirled. As if cursed to his belly, the detective began crawling, nose to the earth, with sulfurous swamp gas making him nauseous. The mosquitoes feasted upon his flesh while lizards and rats scampered away from the noise of his gasping. *Keep crawling,* he told himself. *Keep crawling. Find the sniper. Save the girls.* And then came a sickening, soft thud, thud, thud. It was one of the most horrifying reverberations on earth, the sound of an alligator on the prowl for a meal.

Knowing to lie still, as if lifeless, the detective held his breath and avoided eye contact, hoping the beast would change direction.

The hissing, acidic breath hit the cop in the face, the heat belying the cold-bloodedness. Jaws open, ready to rip him to pieces, the alligator seemed to have no fear of man, as if the laws of nature had been suspended. Beauchamp raised his pistol and aimed at the snout, discerning how the bullet might proceed to the tiny brain. He hesitated to pull the trigger, however, worried that the sniper would see the flashpoint.

The gator whipped its weapon of a tail, smashing the man's thigh. Blood spurted from his bullet wound with such pain that Beauchamp lost consciousness for a moment, and reawakened to a recurring horror. The monster hissed, the sound vibrating as if traveling back in time to the first instance of a beast devouring a human being. Beauchamp resigned himself to becoming sustenance for the reptile, saying a prayer that was merely a whimper, and then the merciless beast, for reasons or instincts unknown, turned its toothy face away from the detective. Thud, thud, thud, the gator disappeared into the darkening vegetation.

Beauchamp waited awhile, making sure it was really gone and not playing a trick, and then he resumed his crawl toward the poisonwood, hoping his direction was accurate. He kept his head low, almost scraping the ground, trying to be as silent as possible. Other alligators were near, and death was everywhere. *Keep on crawling.*

A rat snake slithered to his left, followed by various panicked creatures, all scurrying in the same direction, which the detective now recognized as east. The animals knew that the wildfires were not contained.

Keep on crawling . . .

A speckled log blocked the muddy path to the poisonwood, and the detective paused for a few moments, catching his breath, trying to decide: *Should I go over the log or around it?* He watched a possum scuttle over with ease, and thought he'd do likewise. Beauchamp pulled himself halfway over the soft log, and it began to expand and contract as if breathing. *What on earth?* The log began moving, slowly slithering. It was a giant python, angered by the weight of a man on its back, and it suddenly coiled to attack the rider.

"No, no," Beauchamp said, rolling into the grass. His wounded leg smashed a jut of limestone. "God . . ." he murmured, and the pain made him unconscious again.

Hungry for flesh and blood, the python flicked its forked tongue near the man's helpless, dying face.

Chapter 75

Tongues of lightning hissed near the kayak, causing the young women to sway and almost topple into the moat.

Regaining her balance, Mia said, "Don't look at me like that."

Joan glared. "Like what?"

"Like that. All pissy."

"Well, Miss Valedictorian, you forgot to bring paddles. I'm no expert, I don't have statistics, but it seems to me that kayaks need paddles."

Mia muttered, "Snarky is so twentieth century."

"Kayaks had paddles in the twentieth century."

"So pissy and snarky. Did you remember to bring anything for the journey? Bottled water? No, that was me. Bug repellent? Me again. Energy bars? Me, thricely."

A flash of lightning brightened the moat for a moment, showing a legion of shadows swimming beneath the surface. The young women were so busy glaring at each other that they failed to notice the dangers.

"We can row with our hands," Mia said. "The island is only forty feet away, max. A few strokes and we're there."

Joan wiped her sweaty brow and shivered. "You're crazy if you think I'm dipping my hands in that water. I need my hands to become a painter."

"You only need one hand," Mia said, reaching into the murk. "We can do this. Reach down on the other side and row. I don't see any gators or anything. Besides, the creatures are more afraid of us than we are of them."

Chapter 76

The serpent's eyes were blinded by a milky-white shroud, the molting skin like a mask upon the python's face; and yet it still managed to hunt its prey.

Beauchamp awoke into a nightmare, his own eyes widening in terror. The python flicked its tongue just a few feet away. Beauchamp ached to shoot the beast between those shielded eyes, but his pistol was out of reach and any move to retrieve it could incite the snake to strike.

The detective played dead, white raincoat like a burial cloth, and then a scream arose in the wind, followed by another scream.

The python turned its storm-pummeled head, unable to locate the scent of man, so it blindly flicked its tongue, opened its mouth, and lashed out—barely missing the detective's neck. Enraged, the python struck again, fangs chomping on grass and leaves and liquid air that did not have the sweet taste of blood. The serpent lashed out a final time—smacking into limestone and hissing as if to curse the whole world—and then flick, flick, flick, the hungry monster tasted something in the wind. And it began to slither away, like a nightmare in slow motion, toward the moat and the girls.

Extending his hands into the muddy grass, not sure what else might be lurking to bite him, Beauchamp reached around in the festering Everglades, writhing in pain, until he found his pistol. "Thank God. Now it's a fair fight again." He continued onward through sawgrass and thistle, losing more strength while following the serpent. *Keep crawling. Keep crawling.*

The storm howled like a sky full of beasts, and the long-suffering cop dragged himself toward the poisonwood, following the path of the python, leaving a trail of blood that would certainly attract other predators, and suddenly the wind subsided and the rain stopped. For several moments, the storm ceased. And yet there was no silence. Slither, slither, the whole world seemed to be slithering.

"Help me! Help me!"

Shrieks of agony resounded in the wilderness. They were the death cries of a man, a man being eaten alive by an alligator.

Chapter 77

While the sniper was being devoured by a gator, Joan and Mia maneuvered their kayak across the moat, rowing with their arms, rowing wildly enough to scare away most of the shadows beneath the windblown surface.

"Ouch!"

Joan yanked her hand from the water and checked her fingers. "Something bit me."

"Are you bleeding?"

"No. But my hand is all tingly."

Mia tried to reassure her. "Probably just cute little minnows, giving you love nibbles."

"Cute little minnows?" Joan clenched her fist as if she wanted to punch the entire wilderness. "Don't talk to me about cute little minnows and love nibbles. Talk to me about hideous monsters. Venomous, poisonous, blood-mouthed monsters prowling through the swamp. No, I take it back. Don't talk to me about that."

Mia glanced in the direction of a poisonwood tree. "Did you hear that?"

Shaking her head, Joan raged in silence.

"I could have sworn I heard something," Mia said. "Over there. Hmm. Oh well. It was probably just my imagination. Let's keep paddling. We're halfway to the island."

The trees, festering with frogs, arose in a chorus of forewarning, a sort of tropical opera of discordant croaking.

"We're going to die," Joan said. "Understand? This isn't some fun adventure. It's a sacrifice. Understand?"

Mia faced her friend while the kayak drifted over a horde of shadows. "We'll be okay. The map came to us for a reason. We're not going to die."

Joan already appeared somewhat dead. Her face was pale and ghoulish, with bruise-colored curls of wet hair strangling her neck like so many snakes. A pitiful moan fell from her lips, and she murmured, "I vowed to help Donna, no matter how dangerous that would be, but I never signed up to be a sacrifice."

The idea of retreating, now that they were so close to the Tree, was repulsive to Joan, and yet she knew enough history to know that sometimes it's best for soldiers to fall back, regroup, and make a better plan. "Let's at least find a place that has phone service," Joan said. "We should give Beauchamp a call. We need someone with a gun out here."

"Are you sure you want to contact him? Isn't he a sicko?"

Joan felt bad for having said mean things about the detective. "He's probably okay. And it's his job to help us."

"Okay," Mia said, looking warily at the water. "Let's turn the kayak around."

The girls lowered their hands into the murderous moat and immediately attracted various teeth and fangs, a whole swarm of hungry beasts—and one larger than the others, with a greater taste for flesh. Truly, a monster was on the move, and Joan would be the first to be dragged into the murk and torn asunder while her face resembled *The Scream*. And Mia, who thought horror stories were harmless fun, would scream and shriek while the creature strangled, chomped, and swallowed her best friend.

However, an instant before the monster attacked, a slant of light broke through the clouds with a wind like a solar flare, blasting the kayak across the moat and lifting it in the air while Joan yelped and Mia flailed, her bonnet flying away. The gust dropped the girls on the island, onto a shore of glistening ferns, where raindrops sparkled like beads of gasoline ready to burst into flame. Everything on the island was breathing, breathing the blazing wind, and the whole place seemed incendiary, ready to combust, with hellish smoke rising from the center.

After catching her breath, Mia said, "What should we do, Joan? Should we explore it, or go home?"

Joan removed the map from her pocket. Hands trembling with both fear and courage, she unfolded the soggy paper. She studied the map for a few moments, muttering to herself, and then put it away. "It doesn't make a lot of sense. The drawings don't seem to be from ground level, but from above. Anyway, now that we're on the island, I guess I'm bound to find out why the Tree is at the center of everything, and how it might connect with Donna. You stay here, Mia."

"By myself?"

"Listen. I noticed on the map that there's a faint outline of feathers over the whole place. If this island belongs to the WINGS, then it's the most dangerous place on earth. So I need you to keep watch, okay? And if you see anyone approach the moat, yell your lungs out. And I'll come running back."

Mia was only half listening to that plan, because she'd suddenly noticed, hovering near a path, a shimmering creature like a giant bird, something angelic, and beckoning. *Me? You want me to go?* Mia didn't usually have visions, just confusing dreams, and now she made the mistake of thinking that she ought to explore the island. "Give me the map, Joan."

"What? No."

"Give me the map, and you stay here. You're more of a soldier than I am, so it's your job to do the protecting, while I do the exploring."

There was something in Mia's voice that was more commanding than usual, and although Joan was uneasy with the new plan, she felt obligated to obey. "Here. Take the map. But please stay on the path. Take a quick look around, snap a few pictures, and return immediately. Okay?"

The angel shook its wings and beckoned for Joan to accompany her friend, but the tormented artist missed the sign, and stayed in the kayak on the shore. "Hurry, Mia. Just take a quick look, and then we'll be done."

Digging in the backpack, Mia pulled out a small canister. "Here." She placed it in Joan's hand as if passing along a great power. "Take this."

"What is it?"

"Mace."

Joan almost laughed. "You think a creeper might flirt with me?"

"If so, blind him."

A smoky gust of wind sent Mia on her way, stumbling through a cluster of ferns that were sticky with spider webs. "Augh! All over my hair and face and neck!"

"You okay over there?"

"Yeah, I'm fine."

Mia thrashed at the webs that would not go away, thinking she'd made a catastrophic mistake. She began to choke with tears, feeling a horror that had enveloped many others in the Everglades. Where was the angel? She couldn't see any wings through the branches. However, through a gap in the greenery, Mia saw the winding path. She rubbed her eyes and removed a cobweb from around her neck. "Here I go, Joan! I'll be back in a few minutes!"

"Okay. I'll hold down the fort, um, kayak."

Gulping for air and courage, Mia plunged through the ferns. Her soggy feet found the path and she entered a shady hammock of strangler figs, dogwood, and tamarind. The island smelled of sweat, as if the whole place were nervous. "*Psychtria*," she whispered, noticing a coffee tree among the other limbs. "*Psychtria nervosa.*" The words were drowned by a torrent of wind and rain, causing Mia to run faster. The storm was closer than she expected, and the island was larger, and the path more twisted than shown on the Secret Map. Labyrinthine and dark, the landscape was strewn with dead branches and rotting leaves that covered several pits of quicksand.

The WINGS had prepared the area so that no person could venture this far without being touched. But just to be sure, they'd cast tongues of fire upon the island to ensure that nobody would approach the Tree. The spell was a nonsense prayer—an energy like the splitting of syllabic atoms—made up by the Ninth One years ago, his tongue lolling as if automatically, reversing the order of the universe, at least to the extent allowable. The eight others had joined him, singing the praises of their selves while the shallow ground reverberated and shifted beneath the Tree. And all throughout the island, methane gas now breeched the surface, the hissing rising to ears that refused to hear.

Except the dragon always heard everything, hidden in darkness behind the Tree.

This way, girl. This way.

Mia was drawn to the garden as if called by the sweetest voice. She pushed through brambles and more spider webs, thrashing her way out of shadows and into another sort of murkiness. A column of smoke arose in front of her, dancing skyward, veiling the glow of forbidden fruit, and yet Mia recognized the Tree. She knew it from the map, and felt it in her soul. The girl was instantly thrilled by a feeling of magic, murder, and grace that filled the hazy clearing with every dimension of history and future.

"Oh. My. No!"

Chapter 78

Beauchamp crawled on his belly through biting grass and thistle, slowly pursuing the python. The man realized he was dying, his blood seeping into the Everglades, and yet he was committed to saving the lives of the girls. His final plan, his last act on earth, would be to shoot the snake before it reached the moat. *Inflict a mortal wound*, he thought. *It must be mortal.* The tail disappeared, and Beauchamp worried that he'd lost the beast. He reached out with red hands and clenched the ground more firmly, dragging himself forward.

Tongue flicking, the python knew that something delicious was near. The beast slithered past the remains of a sniper, paused for a moment to offer the corpse a disgusted hiss—and continued toward the moat.

Joan was reclining in the kayak on the shore of the island, feeling relatively safe and watching what shouldn't have been there. And yet, there it was: a happy otter. The creature's webbed feet were like wings, allowing the otter to fly in an underwater sky like an acrobat, making fools of the cumbersome shadows all around. The moat was a heaven for the innocent otter, and the ease of his movement made Joan feel light and relaxed—in the deadliest place on earth—and she was just about to offer up a prayer of thanks.

Oh, God… Please. NO!

The python's grinning head arose from the moat, blind eyes staring and tongue flashing like a dark flame.

Joan's face became somewhat like *The Scream*—and yet our heroine was loathe to set a bad example for all the lower forms of life, so she kept the hysteria to herself and instead shouted encouragement to the otter. "Swim for your life! Go!"

The otter seemed to laugh in the face of death, even as massive jaws opened and attacked. The first strike missed by a splashing inch, compelling Joan to shout, "Swim away! Make your escape!" However, the acrobat whirled around the python as if playing with a toy. Teasing and chattering, the otter made the snake lunge awkwardly in its blindness. The front paw of the otter scratched the face of the python, tearing away a veil of old skin, perhaps a fatal mistake. Now the monster could see its prey, could see what was laughing at him, and instantly clamped upon the otter's paw. The captive mammal shrieked and flailed while the python swam toward shore to find a better place to kill and swallow.

Joan was tempted to go completely numb, allowing the horror to have control. *What am I doing out here? What am I doing?*

The serpent raised its neck above the water while the otter squirmed. In a flash of green lightning, the python appeared to be less of a snake and more of a dragon. To Joan's mind, it appeared to be a devil, some sort of power or principality rising from a murky hell.

And she maced it.

Aiming for the exposed beady eye, Joan expelled the Mace with precision.

Unblinking, the monster stared into Joan's soul with a coldness that seemed dispassionate, and yet a reaction was building, not so much in response to the Mace, but because of the girl's edgy willfulness. The beast hissed and raged, its neck lashing wildly, dropping the otter with a splash. Now the serpent wanted to slither on shore and kill the girl, its tongue and fangs flashing as if already tasting her flesh.

"Joan," a voice rasped.

The girl shook violently, terrified that a snake could talk.

"Joan."

Aiming the canister again, the girl shot the remainder of Mace. Most of it sailed above the head but some hit the eye and nostrils. Incensed, the reptile made a noise that sounded like a roar, then lowered its neck and disappeared beneath the surface of the moat.

"Joan."

The voice sounded like death. Or like someone dying. The girl wondered if the voice was real, or perhaps emanating from her own mind.

"Over here."

Joan glanced across the moat and saw a slight movement on the mainland. A bloody hand appeared above the grass, swaying and clutching a pistol.

"Take this. Joan, take this."

The voice belonged to Beauchamp. Face-down, spent of blood and unable to crawl any further, the detective rasped, "Take the gun."

"Detective? Is that you?"

The man's breathing was like a whirlwind of suffering. "Take. The gun."

"Detective? Is that really you? Hello? Who's in the bushes?" Joan raised the empty canister in a grandiose bluff. "If you're messing with me, I'll hurt you."

Smiling in his agony, Beauchamp was glad to have taken a bullet to save this girl. He gritted his teeth, pushed the ground with his left arm, and tried to rise to his knees, thinking he could toss the pistol across the moat. He knew Joan would be facing more danger. "It's me," he said. "I'm here. To help you." The pain in his thigh was excruciating, and he could not stand.

Joan leaned forward in the kayak, staring across the water. "Detective! What happened? What's wrong?"

"I've been shot. I'm bleeding to death."

The words tore at Joan's heart, and she felt attuned to her mother, the nurse, the healer; and she was determined to save the detective's life. "Hold on!" She got out of the kayak and pushed it into the water. "I'll row over there! I'll stop the bleeding!" The girl climbed back in, almost falling as it surged ahead. She sat and lowered her hand over the side, into the dark water as if reaching toward hell. Joan wanted to instantly withdraw her hand, go back to shore, and not try anything heroic. After all, Beauchamp must have called for help on his police phone.

"Did you call for help?" she asked.

No response.

"Detective? Are you still with us?"

No response.

Joan forced herself to keep working her hand against the darkness, stroking above the shadows, maneuvering the kayak toward the other side.

In the middle of the moat, she was greeted by a serpent's head and neck. The beast was definitely something more than a normal python, rising like a sea monster, like something created by mad scientists.

Joan screamed and tried to paddle away, but the beast was faster, circling around and hissing just inches from her face, hissing as if breathing steam. The girl raised her hands, palms like pale shields. The monster opened its enormous, murderous jaws to swallow her down—his flickering tongue approaching. The girl kept her hands outstretched, expecting the sting and gulp of death at any moment, when the serpent suddenly turned and descended into the deep again.

"Joan, help me!"

What?

"Joan!"

A female voice called from the center of the island, the sound deadened by wind and rain and thick vegetation, and yet Joan knew instantly it was the voice of her friend.

"Mia! What's wrong? Where are you?"

"I'm at the Tree! I need the Mace! Hurry, help!"

The Mace was all gone. But Beauchamp had a gun. If only Joan could regain her courage and start rowing again. *I don't think I can. I can't. Oh God, please help me. I can't, I can't.* Reaching into the moat,

Joan winced as if already bitten by an eel or something worse. Then a huge shadow approached her fingers, and she yanked her hand from the water.

"Joan, help me!"

Dark spots of light swam in the air in front of Joan's eyes. Wobbling, she knelt in the middle of the kayak, afraid of fainting dead into the moat.

"Joan," the detective whispered. "Catch."

Groaning, Beauchamp tossed the pistol as far as he could—the only chance that Joan had of saving Mia.

The pistol splashed into the water exactly where the serpent had descended. The weapon sunk to the depths where it couldn't possibly be retrieved.

Mia's voice was beyond hysterical. "Hurry, Joan! Take the path to the Tree! Please, please, I need your help!"

Chapter 79

"We're too late," Rico said, driving the van slowly past the fruit market. "We're too late for milkshakes. The place is already closed."

Dontey grimaced, perplexed by his friend. "You carjacked my ride and drove like a maniac down here to Snakeville, obliquely mentioning a secret map, and there's a fire burning out west, and the sky is all weird, and you want to stop for a milkshake?"

Rico kept driving. "I was hoping the girls would be here. If they were following the map, they might have stopped here before going to the old military base. Dang. We're too late."

Watching a goat fall to the ground in the petting zoo, followed by another fainting goat, Dontey felt a foreboding that he and Rico would be the next to drop. *Should I mention the thing about the Gateway Garden? Should I let him know that I beat up a freak, and his friends are probably out for revenge?*

Turning onto the road leading deeper into the Everglades, Rico pointed at the sky. "Look. Green lightning. Some people call it Saint Elmo's Fire."

Dontey wasn't sure he wanted to see fire in the sky, something his father had preached about many times, but he looked up and said, "Oh, that's cool."

"Yeah, it only happens during hurricanes."

"But it's not even raining now."

"I know. And the wind hasn't been terrible. But . . ." Rico raised his finger like a gun. "That seems like an eye."

"Where? Where do you see an eye?"

"Directly above us."

Chapter 80

When Mia had traveled the dreamlike path to the center of the island, a deep silence had taken root in her soul. The rattlesnakes stopped rattling, the clouds stopped thundering, and the girl stood in quietude as old as Eden. Approaching the Tree, she whispered, "It's real."

Silvery raindrops glazed the flesh-colored branches of the Tree and gave shine to the fruits. There weren't many fruits, however, only a dozen or so, sickly purple-red and drooping like oblong bruises.

"Yuck."

And yet the desire to partake was immediate. The girl glanced around warily, feeling eyes peering at her, knowing that every move was being monitored. But that wouldn't affect her decision. The urge to indulge was irresistible.

"Take and eat."

Resistance would require a will that Mia did not possess, and graces far beyond the Everglades.

"Snake and sneak."

The words hissed out of her own mouth as if flicked by a forked tongue, and while Mia reached for the nearest bruise of fruit, her spirit discerned the moment for what it was: life or death.

And she heard Joan screaming in the moat.

At first Mia ignored her friend's cry. After all, the fruit was at her fingertips. She could almost taste it, the sweet suffering of the whole world, right there.

"Take and eat."

"Snake and sneak."

And more screaming.

Hold on, Joan. While Mia formed the first word to shout a promise of rescue, to assure her friend that she was not alone, a dragon stepped out of the darkness from behind the Tree. Wearing a bloody mouth like an ancient mask, the Komodo smiled and plodded in its heavy, slithering way, closer and closer, plodding and slithering.

Information about the dragon preyed upon Mia's mind. *The Komodo is the largest lizard on earth, a living dinosaur. The dragon has long serrated teeth that can tear off huge chunks of flesh. Its claws can puncture my ribcage and rip out my heart.*

The monster crept toward the girl, its long yellow tongue tasting the air for her warmth. The Komodo was covered by an occult design of dark scales, a mosaic of malice. Ten feet long and three hundred pounds of hunger, the dragon could actually devour her.

"Go away," Mia stammered. "Go away."

The dragon attacked like it was personal between him and the girl, like a blood vendetta, the forked tongue flicking as if no amount of death would satisfy it.

Mia knew that climbing the Tree was her only chance of survival. She turned away from the monster, grabbed a low-hanging branch, and began pulling herself up with a primitive strength that surprised her. Muscles in one accord, the girl reached for a higher branch and continued to climb. The Tree was sturdy and much taller than the dragon was long, so Mia took refuge near the crown, her heart beating wildly. Glancing down through the leaves, she could barely glimpse the drooling face of the dragon while it grinned up at her. *At least it doesn't have wings,* she thought. *At least it can't fly.*

The Komodo stood on its hind legs, poking its bloody face through the low branches.

Don't faint, Mia told herself. *If you faint, you'll die.* The smoky air made her cough, and while the dragon stared with murderous eyes, Mia lost her strength, slipped, and nearly tumbled. She cursed and screamed for help while trying to regain her balance. She gripped the branches more tightly, leaned down, and spat at the serpent. "Get the hell out of here!"

The dragon flinched as if struck by fire, and Mia felt her spirit soar. She prayed with a smile of victory: *Thank you! Thank you!*

And the dragon began climbing the Tree.

Chapter 81

Dear Reader, you may be muttering: "I won't retire in Florida. Yikes! I'm gonna retire in Minnesota (far away from tropical reptiles) and become one of those mystics who lives in a hollowed-out frozen tree. That's Heaven on earth!"

Dear Reader, if you are finished muttering about your retirement, then I must tell you: several of your favorite characters in this story are about to die. Some will go to Heaven. And some will have to stay in Florida.

Chapter 82

Beauchamp lay in the bloody grass while the creatures of the Everglades crawled all over him, and around him, fleeing eastward to avoid the approaching fire. Some flames had already made it to the island, raging through tunnels of limestone suffused with methane. Smoke billowed out of a hundred crevices, and red flashes shot up to join the lightning.

The detective focused all his energy on Joan. Her burden, he knew, was beyond human effort. To retrieve the gun and save her friend, she must dive into hell. *Do it, Joan. Dive.*

Eyes wide, staring down into the murk, Joan felt invisible fangs of terror chewing up her mind, the venom spreading toward her heart. Sitting numbly in the kayak, she was unable to make the leap.

So it would take a miracle—or a serendipitous act of nature—in the form of a gust of wind that suddenly toppled Joan out of the kayak and into the water, forcing her to dive. Down the girl plummeted with her arms outstretched, fists clenched to repel an attack. A grinning gator almost made the girl scream and drown, and a scattering of eels made Joan bite her lip. The blood tasted cold and deathly, and down she plunged.

The awaiting python, illumined by intermittent lightning, formed a constricting circle around the gun. Joan's eyes grew wide while she sank toward the circle of death, and she was tempted to change directions, to propel herself up to the surface, and yet she continued drifting down to the center of the snake. Welcoming her arrival, the monster tightened its body, closing the circle to catch the girl in its constriction. Joan hovered for a moment and thought about Donna adrift in the lagoon at Apocalypse Island, how the murdered body was so like her own. *Did Donna find peace before she died? Did she do something good at the end?*

Descending to save her friend, Joan entered the circle of snake, its coils gripping her while she reached for the gun. Flames sizzled in the water with an upsurge of methane gas, and the girl's fingers grasped the warm handle of the pistol. Now if only she could wriggle away from the murderous embrace.

I'm stuck! I'm stuck!

Joan knew the waterlogged gun would fire one shot only, and then be jammed and useless. Suffocating, while the serpent wrapped itself around her entire body and opened its mouth, Joan decided to use the one shot to kill the beast.

Forgive me, Mia. Please forgive me for not saving you. To save her own life, Joan aimed the pistol between the long fangs and began squeezing the trigger.

Beauchamp discerned she needed more help, and he convulsed in the grass as if taking another bullet. He saw himself leave his body, rising in a flash, weightless and agile like something winged, and he immediately descended into the moat. He saw the struggling Joan making her move, ready to fire the one shot. *No*, he told her, *Mia must live, no matter what*. Quicker than a trigger, Beauchamp wrapped his bloodstained coat around the serpent's head, causing Joan to pause until the beast began to unravel.

Saving the shot, Joan squirmed away from the serpent, kicking her feet—not like someone being chased, but like someone giving chase—and surged through the water toward a sky that was no longer eerie but golden. The eye of the storm had opened over the island, allowing diffused sunlight to fill the girl's vision. Breaking the surface of the moat, surrounded by wisps of smoke, Joan splashed and dragged herself onshore. Slipping on mud while trying to stand, she scrambled forward, weapon in hand.

Resurrection ferns and purple roses lined a hazy path into the jungle, and Joan found a way toward the Tree. Snakes were everywhere in the slick green shadows, but she blotted them out of her mind, charging forward to save her friend.

Mia screamed again, "Help me!"

The path wound through strangler figs, royal palms, and tropical vines that grabbed at Joan's legs, slowing her down and tripping her, and the girl realized it would take several more minutes to reach the clearing. She called out, "Hold on, Mia! I'm almost there!"

"Hurry! It's biting me!"

A thunder of wings approached in the sky like another dragon descending. Hearing the tumult, Joan looked up through a blur of branches, caught a glimpse of the helicopter, but couldn't see who was flying it.

The Ninth One slowed the copter and made it hover at the edge of the tempest. He smiled the same ghoulish grin that had masked men's faces since the first murder, and then said to his companion, "I am an orphan."

"That's nice," the new girl replied.

"Yes. And here we are, in the original chaos that swirled around the genesis of earth."

"What?"

"Look, my love. Down there is the future of the end. Do you see the Tree?"

"Where?"

"In the middle of that island."

"Hmm. I see something, but we're still too far away. Can't you fly closer?"

"This dragon can fly anywhere," the Ninth One boasted, his voice reverberating as if vaulting out of the helicopter and into the sky. "But we need to land here."

The girl's heart sank. "And walk through the swamp?"

"Just a little ways."

"And how will we cross the moat?"

Grinning like the cleverest man or beast, the Ninth One pressed a button on the control panel. A bridge began rising from the dark water, clean and gleaming stainless steel. "Look at that," the Ninth One said. "Is it good to be the king, or what?"

The girl nodded and felt a sudden urge. She reached out and pressed another button on the panel. "What does this do?"

Gunfire erupted from the helicopter toward Beauchamp's blood-soaked body.

"Oh dear," the girl said. "There seems to be a corpse near the moat."

The Ninth One laughed. "He was known to us. And if you touched him, my love, then bless you."

"And what about the trespasser? I see a purple-haired girl, running and glowing in the smoke. Now she disappeared."

The Ninth One re-aimed the copter's guns. "When you see that witch again, press the button."

At that moment, a disembodied voice called over the system, "Identify yourself!"

Ignoring the voice, the Ninth One said to his goddess, "Look. You have a clear shot at Joan. Touch her heart with fire."

"Identify! Now!"

The girl leaned over and asked nervously, "Shouldn't we respond to that?"

"Not yet. First touch Joan with fire."

She who'd be a killer queen stared into the soulless eyes. "Who are you? Really?"

"IDENTIFY!"

"Everyone knows who I am," the Ninth One said.

Expecting the lieutenant at the military base to give him a ten-second countdown, and thinking it would be fun to wait until three (or two or one), and thinking his bravado would be impressive to the new Eve, the man who could not wait to eat of the Tree was absolutely floored when a rocket flashed up from the base and blasted through the helicopter. The missile obliterated the Ninth One's body and blew his mind to the depths of darkness, taking his goddess with him.

* * *

"Dang!" Rico exclaimed. "Dang, Dontey! You see that?"

"Yeah, some sort of fire in the sky! And now it's falling!"

Stomping the gas pedal, Rico drove the van down the road leading to the military base, accelerating to maximum speed. "If the girls are here, we need to get them out of here. Now!"

Snakes and lizards fleeing the fire lost their lives in thump after thump beneath the wheels, but Rico did not swerve, saying, "I hate to kill those things, but I can't slow down."

A large snarling possum was the next thing crushed. "Oh, man. Should I slow down?"

"Go," Dontey said. "Faster! Faster!"

* * *

Joan stood in a clearing, wondering about the explosion in the sky. *Crazy thunder . . . or what?* The rain pelted down like sparks upon the island. *Where's the Tree? Where's Mia?* Bodies of rising smoke began dancing like ghosts, taking over all visibility. Joan marched forward while a ghost shifted its shape, becoming a many-winged spirit, a flaming seraph. *How can I get through this?* The girl tried to keep her courage while more devilish forms appeared around her, rising from the fiery earth.

"Help! Joan! I'm bleeding! The dragon has me in its mouth!"

Those words made Joan sick to her stomach. Her hands trembled so much that she almost dropped the pistol.

"The dragon's killing me! It's killing me!"

Wishing her soldier father was at her side, Joan took a deep breath—*There's nothing else to do*—and lunged into the smoke. She entered the ghostly dance, pistol pointed to shoot the dragon. Her father had taught her how to handle a gun, although at the firing range she'd missed the target several times.

One shot now. Make it count.

Squinting, Joan could not see through the smoke. *Where's the Tree?* She leapt across a billowing fissure hissing from the earth. The Tree remained hidden, shrouded by many specters all swirling with soot and sparks. The wildfire had fully arrived, and the methane cloud was rising from underground, ready to explode. Joan wiped the ashes and moisture from her eyes and marched forward, but the shifting seraph kept her enfolded in suffocating wings.

* * *

"Hold on!" Rico drove the van off the road and into sawgrass. "Crap!" The van hit a limestone pothole, teetered, and almost got stuck.

Dontey yelled, "Dude! This van isn't a four-wheel drive! You can't drive it through the Everglades!"

"Sure I can," Rico said, veering around a palmetto tree. "It's mostly solid out here. Mia explained how it's mostly rock."

The van sloshed through a mud hole, slid sideways, straightened, and just missed an alligator.

"Dude! We're gonna get stuck and eaten by gators!"

"No, we're good."

Another mud hole, another alligator near miss.

Dontey yelled, "We're not good! Can't you see the gators?"

"What do you want me to do?"

The question was complex. Dontey considered ordering his friend to stop and turn around, but then his mind refocused on the dream of knighthood and how it was in his blood to be heroic. He answered, "We'll keep looking for our friends."

* * *

The seraph of smoke had Joan surrounded, and the girl lost her sense of direction. She called out, "Mia, where are you? Mia, answer!"

There was no answer, just a sizzle of fiery rain and a growl of wind. In Joan's panicked imagination, her best friend was already gone, gorged to death by the dragon.

* * *

Lieutenant Petrov squinted, trying to discern the blurry words on the trespassing van. "PRIMITIVE . . . HOLY," he muttered. Red ants had swarmed the command center and were biting his face, so Petrov slapped himself and activated another missile. "Only a hostile would be out here today. It must be another hostile." Protocol prevented him from launching missiles at land vehicles because those were to be stopped by snipers. However, all but one of the snipers had been sent away to fight the fire, so Petrov watched to see if the remaining one did his job. The guy hadn't been answering the radio and seemed out of position. *Shoot the tires! Shoot the windshield! Why aren't you shooting?* The van kept on going, plowing through the river of grass like an all-terrain vehicle. The lieutenant slapped at the ants biting his neck. *The hostile is heading toward the wreckage. I better take it out.* He reached to flick a switch, his mind fully activated to do his duty, what the Higher-Ups paid him to do. And yet his finger trembled. The next moment filled the lieutenant's mind with a million decisions—memories from his entire life—all presenting themselves like a horizon of hovering rain. Some of the droplets were light and silvery, others dark and destructive.

"Come in, missile command."

The voice was unfamiliar and the terminology incorrect. Petrov wondered if it originated from the van, and he did not respond. Was it a trick or an innocent mistake? The torrents of rain gathered in a massive gust and formed a whirlwind, twisting and shooting embers everywhere. *PRIMITIVE . . . HOLY . . . Is the van weaponized? Are they acting alone, or part of a larger plan?* The lieutenant checked the camera monitors to see if anything was happening near the Tree, but the screens were flickering. *Maybe I need to go out there.* With an army of ants on his body, and feeling a venom-induced shock, Petrov made up his mind to abandon the base. He left the command center while the whirlwind became all fire.

* * *

Joan's lungs ached for air. Caught in the wings of a dark angel, she could not see the fiery tornado as it approached the island, and yet the howling winds and squeals of fleeing creatures were enough to make the girl fall to her knees. Where the WINGS had chanted their rituals, Joan began to sob and cry out.

"Just give up," a voice seemed to say. "Just scream and scream and give up. After all, that is the answer to this world. There is no escape, and no rescue, and nothing to do but just scream and give up."

To which Joan responded, *What? No. To hell with that. I'm here to save Mia.*

Rising and pointing her pistol into the foul breeze, the girl leapt forward and ran straight through the false angel. With tears in her eyes, Joan could barely see Mia's limp body dangling from an upper branch of the Tree while a Komodo dragon gnawed on her bleeding foot.

"Mia, no," Joan whimpered. "Don't be dead. Don't be dead!"

Joan felt utterly alone and helpless, and there was no human skill in her possession by which she could make everything right. In a time and place worse than any nightmare, Joan's mission seemed lost in a final cry. And so goes life, so goes history, the ancient death stinging despite all the heroic words of literature.

And Joan of the Everglades pulled the trigger.

Chapter 83

The whirlwind transformed the moat into a ring the color of blood. Heat rising, rain falling, flocks of birds and creeping things everywhere, Beauchamp saw it all in his death, including a white chariot appearing out of the mist. Two ministering angels climbed out, and were no longer angels, just guys that he'd harassed.

"It's that detective," Dontey said, rushing to his side. "Hey, Beauchamp."

"Is he dead?" Rico asked.

Dontey searched for a pulse, checking the wrist and then the neck. "I'm afraid we're too late. He's gone."

"Poor guy. We better bring him to town," Rico said. "We better bring him to a morgue."

Eyeing the approaching whirlwind, Dontey said, "We'll be in a morgue, too, if we don't hurry. Grab his arms. I'll get his legs. Lift!"

The young men carried the detective to the back of the van, and Beauchamp, deep in his death, began dreaming again.

He was a bullet of another fire, passing through the branches and leaves of the island into the center of the dragon's skull. The great serpent hissed, letting go of Mia's leg, and fell to the ground beneath the Tree. Its cursed belly crashed upon twisted roots, breaking a rib and puncturing its heart.

Good shot, Joan thought. *We killed it! We killed it!*

Near the crown of the Tree, Mia gasped, "Joan?"

"Mia? You're alive! You're not dead!"

"Barely alive. Barely not dead."

Coughing for air, Joan climbed a lower branch. "Mia, we need to hurry. This place is burning up."

"Okay." Mia began slipping down, wincing in pain. "I can't hold on. I'm falling."

Joan climbed another branch. "Put your good foot on my shoulder. Put the pressure on me, Mia. Don't worry. I'll get you down safe."

The bruised fruits fluttered in the breeze, ready to fall. Dark ooze dripped from the rottenness, and Joan wondered how anyone could be tempted to eat such death. And yet her hand reached out for a moment. *Take and eat. Join with us.* Joan shook her head violently—*No!*—and warned her friend, "Don't touch that putrid fruit! Mia, even if it looks good to you, don't touch it or we'll never get out of here!"

Bacteria, venom, and loss of blood all worked against Mia, making her nauseous and dizzy. The smoke compounded the problem, and halfway down the Tree, Mia was unable to make a final effort to escape. Gripping the branches, she said, "Rest. Must rest."

The whirlwind of flickering debris was nearly upon them. Sparks hissed in the girls' hair while the fruits of the Knowledge of Good and Evil sizzled as if ready to explode.

"Rest over," Joan said. She grabbed Mia's good foot and pulled, and tugged, and shook her whimpering friend from the Tree. Mia fell on Joan's shoulders, and both women tumbled to the ground. Warm, red rain pelted them, along with ashen remnants of the wilderness—scorched plants, flowers, trees, fur, and skin—all falling upon the failed Eden.

"I want . . ." Mia moaned, "sleep."

Face to face with the dead dragon, which didn't seem completely dead, Joan said, "Let's go, Mia. We need to get up. Now."

Mia closed her eyes to the smoke and fire. "Sleep."

"Yes, whatever you want," a charming voice said. "You, too, Joan. Whatever you want. Whatever makes you happy."

The charming voice filled the wind with an incantation that seemed to arise from the dead dragon's tongue. *"To thine own self, for thine own self, choose thyself."*

The words sounded good and true and beautiful. And they presented themselves to Joan as being logical, too. After all, the realistic choice was to leave Mia behind and save her own skin. Joan stood and heard the words, "Yes, whatever you want. Name it and claim it. Look!" Joan could see a blurry vision of Savannah in the smoke, and herself graduating from the College of Art and Design.

"To thine own self, for thine own self, choose thyself."

The incantation, while imitating music, was not music in the highest. And yet it seemed to be the *IS*, the *IS* of all power.

"To thine own self! For thine own self!"

The temptation grew stronger for Joan to flee and leave her friend. The voice said it was the ethical thing, the wise thing to do. Savannah grew brighter in the fire, and Joan could see a hundred of her paintings hanging in galleries across the country. She'd be rich and famous. She'd have fiery lovers. She'd become immortal.

"To thine own self! For thine own self!"

Savannah became London, and Athens, and Tokyo, and Rome. And then nothing but the burning dream of the WINGS. It was not *IS*. It was not.

"We need to ditch this place," Joan said. "C'mon, Mia."

"Can't move. You go."

Gently touching Mia's cheek, Joan said, "Try to stand. Use me for support. Like a three-legged race. C'mon, let's get you home."

Mia gasped, "Can't move. Just leave me."

Joan put her arms under Mia's shoulders and lifted. Like a soldier carries a fallen comrade, like her father saved a man before catching a bullet in the neck, Joan carried her friend above the grinning dragon, across the billowing fissures, and through the furnace of false angels.

"Okay," Mia said, "going home. Safe now, safe . . ."

Giant serpent, Joan thought, staggering upon the path that led to the kayak. *Watch out for the monster. We have no Mace and no gun.* She stumbled and dropped Mia near a strangler fig. "That's okay," the dying girl said. "Leave me. Let me burn."

"What happens to you happens to me, *mon amie*. Give me your hand."

Joan lifted her again and continued stumbling forward through the vines and brambles. "We'll get off this island, Mia. Hold on, hold on." Reaching the resurrection ferns, Joan nearly collapsed, hyperventilating, thinking her bloody arms couldn't carry her friend any further. *I need to keep going. I can't, but I need to. Just one step at a time. One step . . .* And it seemed like she was being helped by some invisible presence, and she heard the slightest whisper of words, "and deliver us." The words made Joan feel invincible, like she could do anything, so she forced a smile and took a step forward into the resurrection ferns, and her foot immediately kicked a rattlesnake.

The rattler's strike would mean double death. If the fangs bit Joan's leg, both women would fall to the ground and burn in the whirlwind. Shaking its percussive tail as if summoning spirits, the snake was so entranced in its music that it failed to strike in time. Joan lurched away, carrying Mia through the ferns until she suddenly came to a stop, teetering at the moat's edge.

"Where's the kayak? It should be here. Where is it?"

"Sleepy..." Mia whispered. "Let me sleep."

"There it is!" Joan yelled. "There it is! Oh, crap."

The kayak was in flames and half-submerged.

Knowing it would be impossible to swim across the infested moat, Joan scanned the shoreline for an overturned tree that would allow passage to the other side. She saw a few large trees that had fallen, and scolded them for not falling in a helpful way. "Stupid trees. We hug you. Can't you hug us back?"

"Drop me," Mia whimpered. "I'm fat as a raft. Float across the moat on me."

"Don't be stupid. You're not fat. And no, I'd never use you as a raft."

"You're good, *mon amie*," Mia said, and lost consciousness.

The conflagration worsened, with absolutely no way to escape the burning island. And yet Joan refused to weep, refused to give up, even if the thoughts now occurring to her seemed delusional. *I'll retrieve what's left of the kayak, and I'll make a sail, and I'll fasten Mia to the sail and hoist her into the wind and she'll fly across the moat. That could work. Or maybe . . . we'll simply walk across that bridge that just appeared. What on earth?*

"Mia, look! A bridge!"

"Blow it up," Mia muttered, regaining consciousness. "It's a trick. Angels . . . bad ones, playing tricks."

While Joan dragged Mia toward the bridge, the church van sloshed through steaming waters that were spilling into the moat.

"Is that them?" Rico asked, pointing toward the ring of fire. "I think it's them! Dontey, look over there! Do you see them?"

"I'm not sure. There's too much smoke."

And with a sickening boom, the Tree erupted like a nuclear bomb, the blast shooting up and down and sending the girls flying across the scorching bridge. The guys had to shield their eyes while a geyser of water and methane shot up from the caverns, red steam twisting and hissing, the whole center of the island rising into a hellish pillar of flame.

The van was pummeled by the blast, almost tipping over, and then Dontey and Rico jumped immediately out and rushed forward into the chaos.

"Mia!"

"Joan!"

Surrounded by fire, the young women felt like they were lost and found in a nightmare, and also in a beautiful dream. If they were in Hell, then why did two guys suddenly appear, and appear so glorious? Dontey and Rico shouted their greetings and asked if everything was okay, and their concern was like the loveliest whisper, and they lifted the girls in their arms and carried them to the van.

When everyone was in the vehicle, the guys were shocked by how bedraggled, even dead, their friends looked—hair partially scorched and clothes covered with blood and soot. Rico said, "I'm sorry we didn't get here sooner."

Mia was curled up not far from Beauchamp, and mumbled, "Is he alive?"

The guys were silent, and Joan said, "It feels like the whole earth exploded, and now everything is sinking. Let's go, before we're stuck."

The unspoken word, *forever*, hung in the air like a final threat.

Dontey sat ready at the wheel, no longer allowing Rico to handle the driving. "I've steered this van through many storms. I'll get us through this one." His voice was strong, yet worried about rain-soggy ground. It would be impossible to drive all the way back to the road. "Hold on. Here we go." Dontey turned the van around and accelerated, thinking: *I'll take them as far as I can.*

"Faster!" Rico said, looking back at the burning island. "Get us to the military base!"

Joan tapped Dontey on the shoulder. "Is there a first-aid kit in here?"

"I'm not sure," he said, swerving around a sinkhole. "Check the back panels."

"Okay." Opening the panel on her side of the van, Joan found nothing but songbooks. And so she crawled over Beauchamp's corpse and searched the other side of the vehicle. "Here it is. Good. Disinfectant and clean bandages. Listen, Mia, we have to clean your wound. I have to lift your leg."

"No! Hurts!"

"I'm sorry. I know it hurts. I'm sorry."

The van sloshed through the storm and burning debris while Joan attended to her friend, cleaning the wound and wrapping it. She was terrified that a false move would cause Mia to die.

In a childlike voice, Mia said, "Pain . . . going away."

That's not good, Joan thought. *The venom and poison have taken over. Pain would be a blessing, a sign of life.*

Sputtering, the van made some progress despite the wind gusts battering it and making it swerve toward deepening waters. "Be careful," Rico said, whispering. "We need to get Mia to a hospital. And if we stall, we're all dead."

Paws and claws were everywhere, and wings flapped through clouds of smoke, everything seeking refuge to the east.

The van thumped over a drenched raccoon.

"I wish we could save the animals," Dontey said.

"We're not Noah's Ark," Rico responded, looking at the rearview mirror.

Mia moaned, "I'm dying . . . dragon killed me."

"You're not dying," Joan said, kissing Mia's forehead. "You're going to become a senator, or the President. You're very much alive."

Mia shook her head. "I won't even be . . . a mayor."

"Stay calm. Think good thoughts."

"I can't. I'm dead."

Rico turned toward the back of the van and spoke with a cheerful bravado. "You'll be fine, Freckles. I know you'll be fine. The doctors in Miami know how to deal with snake venom."

"I got bit," she moaned, "by a dragon. Doctors don't know dragons. My foot is . . . dead."

Leaving the passenger seat, Rico crawled into the back and gently knelt beside Mia. Not knowing exactly what to say, he spoke with absolute sincerity. "Mia, you can have my foot."

"Really?" she asked. "You'll give me . . . your smelly foot?"

Rico nodded. "You can have it. I love you."

"You love . . . me," Mia said dreamily. "And I love... my new foot."

Sploosh!

The solution hole was several feet deep. The van almost made it across but became stuck in mud—with an axle hung up on limestone.

Mia whimpered and drifted off to sleep, her face ashen. Joan wanted to hold her and cry, but she shouted an order. "Dontey! Get us out of here! Now!"

Shifting into reverse, and into drive again, Dontey tried to rock the vehicle free. "It's not working," he said. "We're really stuck."

Rico checked his phone and sighed angrily. "No signal. And where is a helicopter when you really need one? I mean—"

"Get out," Dontey said.

"What?"

"Get out, bro. We need to push."

"We? If we're out pushing, who's gonna drive? Huh? Who's gonna drive?"

"Joan is."

The girl hesitated, hovering over her patient. "Me? Drive through the Everglades? I don't think so."

"Listen," Dontey said. "We have about five minutes before the entire place becomes a methane lake of fire."

"A river," Rico corrected him. "The Everglades is a river."

Dontey glared. "Whatever you want to call it—a river, a swamp, a cesspool of death—we need to get out of here."

"Right," Rico said. He opened the side door and jumped into the foul air. "Reeks of burning snake. Ugh. I can't handle the smell of burning snake."

"Okay, I'll drive," Joan said. "How far?"

"All the way to the military base," Dontey replied, adjusting the seat for her. "Don't give the engine too much gas. Keep it flowing steady. Rico and I will get us unstuck. We'll stay outside and keep pushing until you find the road."

"Or I could push," Joan said. "And you could drive."

Dontey shook his head, thinking about how many times he'd pushed a steel sled during football practice. "We each have our gifts. Keep the headlights on low, and try to swerve around the solution holes. If we fall into a deep one—deeper than the one we're in now— we're doomed."

"Great. Put all the pressure on me."

Offering a confident smile, Dontey took her hand. "We're a team, all right? We'll push and you'll save us. Got it?"

Joan nodded, although she wasn't happy about the plan. "Got it."

"Good," he said giving her another smile. "Now I'm out of here."

I can't drive, Joan thought. She squinted out the windshield into the swirling storm. *It's like zero visibility, even with the headlights on.*

"Let's make it happen," Dontey said to Rico, digging his heels in the mud. He shoved his shoulder against the back of the van while his friend lifted the front bumper. The guys were able to move the van slightly, but not enough.

"More gas, Joan! More gas!"

The vehicle spun its wheels on the muddy limestone, but could not escape, while a familiar monster slithered closer and closer to the van, tasting Joan's scent with its forked tongue. The giant python ignored the lizards, rats, possums, and other easy prey, much preferring to feast upon a larger victim.

Dontey and Rico, all muscle and purpose, planted their feet anew in the mud, lowered their centers of gravity, and gave everything they had to dislodge the vehicle. It moved several inches forward, the axle rising with their efforts, and then it fell again.

Wanting to curse, but controlling herself, Joan tried to master the whims of the machine. The van sputtered and ka-thunked, complicating her attempt to figure out the right amount of gas to give it. Joan pumped the pedal a few times, pressed harder, and softer, listening for signs of progress in the revving and spinning of wheels. Smoke and steam swirled, reminding the girl of dark seraphs and ghastly wings, and suddenly a swollen face flashed in the headlights.

"Who is that?" Joan gasped, and watched the man take a step to the side and plummet down a pit. "Wait! No!" Just then the van lurched, backfired, and spun its way forward.

"Go!" Dontey shouted. "Give it gas! Accelerate!"

Joan drove slowly and carefully while Rico jogged beside the vehicle, pushing and shouting, "Faster! C'mon, get it to the road!"

"Yeah, go!" Dontey yelled, standing in place. "Don't wait for me!"

Breathing hard and sweating, the star athlete stayed behind, knowing he could sprint and catch up to the van. His left ankle was stuck in the mud, however, and apparently sinking deeper. Dontey tried to lift his leg while the mud moved higher, reaching over his knee. *What is that? Quicksand?* The eerie sensation was intensified by the fact that his legs were perfectly balanced. Dontey could see his right foot on the wet ground, not sinking. And yet his left leg was invisible—all the way up to his thigh. The pressure became painful, as if the mud was actually squeezing him.

Snake! he realized.

The coiling python worked its way higher. The young man raised his arms like someone praying or giving up while the monster wrapped itself around his waist and chest. The weight made Dontey expel more breath, allowing the python to tighten its grip to crush his ribcage and snuff out his heart.

"Help!" he gasped at the church van. "Help . . ."

The taillights were like eyes, growing smaller and smaller, unable to see the twisting horror around Dontey's body.

Puffing his chest, Dontey concentrated on taking shallow breaths, not allowing the snake to constrict him. He thought about his dream, about being a knight, and how the dragon couldn't be killed. Now the beast lifted its grinning face and flicked its tongue at the victim's forehead—as if marking it with a sign.

The young man thought about his father, the fiery preacher who wielded scripture like the ultimate weapon, but Dontey wasn't as sure about storming heaven with chapters and verses. However, he moved his lips and mouthed some words of Revelation, reached through the coils with his right arm, and grabbed the snake's scaly neck.

The python raged and tightened its hold, cracking two of Dontey's ribs. The pain burned all around his chest and through to his heart. The football player was familiar with pain, and had overcome it many times before, so he ignored the agony of broken bones and continued trying to kill the serpent. "Some of your," he gasped, "own medicine!"

Those words, full of precious air, cost him another rib. And yet Dontey kept fighting like the warrior in his dream, and then, beginning to lose consciousness, he recalled a children's book his mom had read to him, about a young Hercules who'd overcome an attack of snakes.

"You are so not Hercules," the snake seemed to say.

Fainting out of the fallen world, Dontey accepted the fact that he'd be killed and devoured. His death would be just another in the long list of tragedies in the Everglades where killer instincts have their sway.

"Ha! There you are," a man said, marching through the muck. He wore military garb, soaking wet, the darkest green. His face was red and swollen, and he accosted the predator before it could eat its prey. "You were trained to stay in the moat! You're disobeying orders. And that means you must be executed."

The serpent flicked its tongue with cool disdain and hissed.

"Yeah, hiss yourself," the man said, pulling out a pistol and squeezing the trigger. The bullet blasted the DNA-enhanced brain, causing the beast to be both dead and more alive. It flailed around in the foul wind, spitting blood and snapping its jaws.

Dontey wheezed for breath while the undead snake uncoiled from his body and tried to attack the man with the pistol. Tongue like fire, and yet with nothing registering in its brainless skull, the serpent was a writhing, snapping mass of mindless revenge.

The red-faced man aimed his gun again, but fangs sank into his hand before he could fire the shot. *"Nyet!"* The pistol fell in the mud. *"Nyet! Nyet!"* The monster continued attacking the screaming soldier, constricting him, and constricting him, all the way up to his chin.

Dontey watched in horror while the giant python opened its bloody jaws to measure the man's skull for swallowing. *"Nyet! Nyet!"* the guy kept screaming. Dontey wasn't sure about helping someone who screamed in Russian and probably worked with Seth, but he was raised in church and told to give everyone a helping hand, no matter what. "Hold on a sec!" Dontey said. "Just give me one second." He staggered over to the pistol, picked it up from the mud, aimed between the python's eyes, and fired.

"Dang."

He missed the snake's head. But he'd managed to puncture its throat. Red foam sprayed out in a raging hiss.

"Fire again, kid," the man gasped. "Fire again!"

Dontey aimed at its face, but the monster swayed and lashed, causing him to accidentally point the gun at the soldier.

"Don't fire, kid! Don't fire!"

"Fine." Dontey dropped the gun, reached out, and grabbed the beast by its bloody throat. He squeezed with otherworldly force while the creature snapped its hellish mouth shut—and open again—fangs just barely missing the kid. "You can call me Hercules," Dontey said. "Or call me Saint George."

The creature hissed continuously, but quieter and quieter, eventually falling dead in the river of grass.

"*Da.* Good!" The man in military garb picked up his weapon and pointed at the van. The taillights were visible again, as if the vehicle had backed up. "Looks like the holy rollers are stuck over there, halfway to the road."

Then we gotta push, Dontey thought. *Crap.* He wheezed for air, his broken bones burning. He was unsure if this dude would agree to help push, so he asked, "You a good guy? Or a . . . bad guy?"

"I'm Lieutenant Petrov," the guy answered, sloshing toward the van. "Follow me."

Dontey didn't like that command. He wanted to get to the van first, so he could warn the others about the weird soldier. Maybe he was okay, but who knows? Dontey squinted into the murky landscape, trying to discern the fastest way through the mire. And he began running.

Petrov called out after him, "You might want to avoid that solution hole directly in front of you. The one with the big alligator."

"Directly in front of me," Dontey muttered. "Yikes!" He slid to a stop at the edge of the pit and waited, allowing Petrov to lead the way through the natural minefield.

Spooked animals continued to flee, running and slithering while the sound of spinning wheels increased to something like a shriek. "Joan, don't blow out a tire," Dontey muttered. "We don't have a spare." He paused, hoping not to hear a loud noise.

"SNAKE!" Petrov yelled, turning around. "Right next to you—a thirty-footer!"

"What!"

"Just kidding, kid. C'mon, keep marching. Follow me and let me do my job. We're almost there."

Dontey kept marching, but he hated the way Petrov said "let me do my job." It reminded him of a psycho with a rifle—Seth—who thought it was his job to shoot people.

Chapter 84

Seven of the WINGS were down in their bunker, sitting in a semicircle, wearing business suits and no masks, discussing the Ninth One and the destruction of the Tree.

"What a waste," Media lamented, "we didn't get any video of the explosion."

"Just fake it," Banks said. "We can capitalize on this."

"La te da, Lolita ta!" Porn sang while parading through the door. "Why all the funny faces? Wasn't the tempest wonderful? It mussed up my hair all nice."

Weapons flashed a furious look. "The Tree has been taken out."

"Taken out?" Porn asked. "On a date?"

Glaring as if to kill, Weapons said, "Porn, we don't really need you. You're completely disposable."

"Now, now," Technology said. "Relax. We can still move forward with everything."

Weapons pointed a gun at Banks. "The price of gold plummeted today. Did you have something to do with that?"

"I sold a billion ounces," Banks said in a deflated voice. "I tried to stop the distribution of some evidence."

Technology echoed, "Evidence. What evidence?"

"The Murskey girl made a video about us. Apparently, she recorded some discussions, charts and graphs, copies of acquisitions. And the after-party of the last Demon Dance."

Media hissed, "Why wasn't I told about this?"

"Because you can't keep a secret," Banks said. "Donna sent the video to some nuns. They edited it and posted it online. Nobody noticed for a while, but then the video began to spread. I paid to scrub the Internet. I even tried to shut the whole Internet down. But I'm afraid all the money in the world won't keep the video from going viral."

Porn giggled, "Is it a fun movie? Would I be proud?"

Weapons cursed and pointed the gun at Porn's face. "Donna exposed us, and the Tree is gone! Understand? The Tree is gone."

"Hmm," Media said, mulling things over. "Maybe there's a way we could squirm out of this."

"We're dead," Agriculture said. "Word is already out. The video is already out. The Tree was the only thing that could have saved us. Without the Tree, we have no way of knowing what to do, and what not to do!"

"Oh, settle down and eat your wontons." Oil raised his voice from the lowest part of the room. "All is well. We can regroup someplace else. There are other hidden islands, and we can make another Tree."

"I'm finished with trees," Technology said. "You guys can go search for Eden or whatever. I'm going to Amsterdam."

"Oh, take me with you," Porn begged. "Amsterdam is a real paradise! And we can hide there in plain sight."

"Yes, that's a good place for us," Oil slurred, wiping his face. "We should depart soon, after the proper rituals."

"Nobody died and made you king," Weapons said. "Your orders have no weight. In fact, your BP executive caused trouble for us. We almost had you touched for that."

"You almost had me touched? Well, well," Oil said. "Another conspiracy within."

There were murmurs around the semicircle, and some talk of murder.

"Ahem." Banks tried to be the voice of reason. "I agree that we should depart and regroup in a new place. We can change our identities and our accounts. We can survive."

Weapons waved his gun at everyone. "Listen. We'll fight this thing from here. We have plenty of firepower at our disposal. And tons of food. There is no better place than down here. We can get everything accomplished, if we just work together."

Ring! Ring!

The red phone rang, the doomsday landline they'd stolen from the Kennedy Bunker on the other side of the island. Weapons hesitated to answer, while Banks stood and reached out his hand to take the call.

"Hello? Who is this? How much do you want?"

The voice on the other side answered the questions and made Banks tremble, and not only because the voice was emanating from an unplugged, ceremonial phone. Quickly hanging up, Banks gasped for breath as if choking on smoke.

"Spit it out, spit it out," Technology said. "Share with the rest of us."

Not yet able to speak, Banks took several deep breaths, gagging and choking, and then finally rasped, "It was, it was . . ."

"A joke," Porn said, laughing uncontrollably and lunging for the phone. He spoke into it with his most sensual voice. "What are you wearing? Do you want to know what I'm wearing?"

Yuck, yuck, yuck—the most powerful men in the world laughed—yuck, yuck, yuck, yuck!

Suddenly all their phones began ringing, even though it was a rule that phones must be turned off during meetings. The WINGS fluttered around for their various devices and answered at the same time, hearing what sounded like a masked voice on the other side.

"I OWN YOU," the voice said. "And I've already sold you."

There was a long silence before Weapons stammered, "Who . . . are you?"

"The Tenth One."

All the phones went dead.

Thunder rumbled above like rolling tanks, with flashes of red light seeping through the cracks in the concrete. Wobbling in his chair, Weapons contemplated the gun on his lap. "There's a Tenth One? Since when is there a Tenth One?"

Media hissed, "He's already sold us."

"Sold into slavery," Agriculture said. "I can't go back to being a slave."

"Shut up," Oil slurred. "Go back to shutting up."

A booming explosion rocked the abyss as if a whole sky of lightning had fallen upon Apocalypse Island. The WINGS collapsed and crashed to the floor, and then thrashed around to regain their proper places in the semicircle. After a minute of fearful murmuring, and a moment of proud silence, a predatory intonation entered their ritual space.

Click-click, slither, hiss ... The sounds echoed down the walkway, approaching the inner room. Click-click, slither, hiss ... The men heard what must have been an enormous creature descending the secret walkway. It sounded large enough to fill the whole abyss, its presence like the ticking of time or the flickering of all fire—or something worse—an image appeared in each man's mind of a famished dragon with wings of otherworldly flame, the many-fanged mouth breathing steam, closer and closer. Click-click, slither, hiss ...

Hearing the approach of their demise, the most powerful men in the world became impotent, unable to formulate devilish tongues or beckon any earthly manifestations of strength. Their power, which had always been a form of suicide, now became despair incarnate.

"Take, and eat," Pharmaceuticals stammered, offering death from a trembling bottle. Oozing black pills were passed from hand to mouth among the men who wanted to have the full knowledge of evil, while the clicking, slithering, hissing creature made a final descent.

"Sneak, and snake," Weapons gasped, the last words of the cult.

***

A minute later, Renata the cleaning lady was not happy to see such a mess on the floor. She'd always had trouble eradicating the smells from the clubhouse, and now it was much worse. She pushed her clicking, slithering, hissing cart closer to the corpses, then grabbed a bottle of disinfectant and sprayed it over the WINGS while muttering, "*Diablos locos—no más, no más.*"

Chapter 85

Dear Reader, you've made the right decision to eschew doomsday cults.

Good call, my friend. Keep eschewing them.

And also, be careful when driving your car through the Everglades.

Chapter 86

The church van sank into the pit, getting more stuck no matter how Rico strained to push it free. Sweating and murmuring a prayer, he refused to grow faint while palm fronds swirled like broken wings in a whirlwind.

Petrov rubbed his pocked jowls and circled the van, discerning the situation. "*Da. Nyet. Da.* Okay, listen to me," he commanded. "Get everyone out of the vehicle. Now! We're walking to the road."

"One of our friends is hurt," Rico replied, "and one of our friends is dead. They can't walk to the road. And who are you to give orders?"

"I enjoy giving orders," Petrov responded, showing the gun. "I'm all done taking them."

"I saved your life," Dontey said, "and you saved mine. So let's work together to bring everyone to safety. All right? C'mon, push the van."

Strange shapes scampered and crawled through the grass and mud. Some squealed as if laughing at the humans. Petrov pointed his gun at the vehicle. "Do you think I'm a dung beetle? Do you think I can push something that weighs a hundred times more than my mass? Why did you call me a dung beetle?"

"I never said that," Dontey said. "You misinterpreted. All I said was—"

Rico interjected, "We don't have time for this. C'mon, we need to push!"

"Is that right? Hmm." Petrov used the pistol to scratch his rain-dripping, repugnant face. "You think the dung beetle is not worthy of intelligent discussion? You think the dung beetle is just something to be crushed beneath the wheels?"

To Rico's mind, it seemed that Petrov wasn't a real soldier but just another gun for hire, and therefore the best course of action would be to take away his weapon. The thought flashed from Rico's brain to his hand—yes, he would disarm the guy—but then the van window began rolling down, revealing Joan's wild hair and flashing eyes. "We're sinking deeper," she said, "and I can't hear Mia breathing. Hurry, you guys, do something!" She leaned further outside and noticed the man with the swollen face. "Who are you?" she asked.

The lieutenant reached toward the window and grabbed Joan's hand. That seemed a bit scary for a moment, but all he did was gently kiss her knuckles and declare, "Joan of the Everglades, I am Petrov, your humble servant."

"Okay, um, humble servant. Push! Get us out of here!"

"Yes, it will be done," Petrov said. "Do not worry. Your friend will live."

Dontey and Rico hated the romantic way the soldier spoke to Joan, but this wasn't the time for wasting testosterone. Petrov strode to the rear of the van, sat in the mud with his back against the bumper, and while the other guys offered their strength to the cause, he pushed with his legs and arched his back with incredible power. The church van arose from the swampy ground like an airboat and flew forward.

"Go, go, go!" they all shouted, running to catch up.

Petrov shadowed the driver's side window, giving Joan directions. "Veer a little to the right, my dear. There is a stone pathway there." He was a knowledgeable guide, familiar with every inch of the Everglades, and he grinned at the thought of receiving a medal for helping the teenagers escape to safety, but there is such a thing as reaping what one has sown, especially if one has worked for the WINGS, and so Petrov slipped and fell and plunged into a large pit awash with snakes and gators. Typically, snakes and gators don't work well together, but in attacking Petrov they were quite a team.

"Oh, man." Rico leaned over the pit, trying to save the poor guy. "Dude, reach up! Reach up for my hand!"

Dontey leaned over the pit and yelled, "Bro, use your gun!"

The gun had fallen into the mucky water, and Petrov was quickly torn asunder. *Florida . . . nyet good*, were his final thoughts.

Meanwhile, Joan kept driving as fast as she could. Almost to the road, she whispered, "Please, just a little further, just a little further," and the church van that acted like an airboat suddenly succumbed to the gravity of the Glades and splooshed into the deepest solution hole. Joan's face hit the steering wheel and the horn sounded like a death knell.

"Joan!" Dontey shouted.

Rico yelled, "Mia, hold on!"

While the vehicle began filling with water, rats, spiders, lizards, and snakes, the tortured artist unbuckled her seatbelt, brushed the blood away from her eye, and plunged into the back of the van to save her friend. "Mia!" she cried, splashing and reaching out while several animals tried to bite her hands and legs.

Rico sprinted to the van like a hero flying on the wind. He kicked out a window and dove into what had become an aquarium, a cage, and a morgue. His mouth filled with putrid water and he spluttered, unable to call out his girlfriend's name—while Joan searched the other side of the sinking van. "Rico, find her! Don't let her drown!"

Outside in the tempest, Dontey was entranced by what appeared to be two large eyes at the military base, growing larger and larger. "Now what?" He'd had enough of monsters for one day. In fact, he'd had enough of monsters for a lifetime. *Is that another giant python? Or . . . something worse?* While Dontey tried to figure out what exactly it was, and wondered if he could survive another battle to the death, Rico found Mia in the rising water. He held her in his heroic arms, and kissed her (several very gross times) with his muddy face. "I found you, Freckles! I found you!"

Mia didn't seem to be breathing, and while Rico tried to resuscitate her, Joan floated toward the windshield, barely keeping her head above the surface, thinking: *Something's approaching. What is that? Another dragon?*

"It's just a hearse," Dontey muttered to himself when the huge eyes showed themselves to be headlights. "Here comes a hearse to take us all away."

Chapter 87

The long black hearse carried the bodies of Beauchamp and the teenagers out of the burning river of grass. Very slowly, because a slow-moving hearse is more horrifying than a fast one, the deathmobile eventually—at the stroke of midnight—pulled up to Joan's house as if arriving at a funeral parlor.

The hearse driver appeared to be a hellion, like some primitive necromancer who might be dead himself but lives to spirit away the newly departed.

"Oh, please, no!" Joan's mother screamed.

And twenty minutes later, in a more upscale neighborhood, Mia's mom ran frantically to her driveway and flung open the door of the hearse and gazed with terror at the sight within, seeing that her only child, her precious daughter, was not a corpse. Not a corpse! No, indeed, Mia's body wasn't even there. She'd been left behind in the ghostly swamp, festering alone to atone for so much kissing.

Dear Reader, oh my, what an active imagination you have!

Here's what really happened.

The driver of the hearse was like most people in Florida, still learning how to drive, except he had the good excuse of being a giant monk from the fifteenth century. Miraculously, he delivered Mia to the hospital, where a team of surgeons was able to save her life—and save her foot. So she didn't need to borrow Rico's smelly foot after all. Although that would have been strangely romantic.

Brother Bean swerved the hearse around some storm debris, and swerved around some silver SUVs that might have belonged to assassins, and managed to deliver the living bodies of Rico, Dontey, and Joan to their respective homes, where the parents were somewhat freaked out. "Yikes!" every parent exclaimed. But it wasn't that big of a deal because the kids had texted them as soon as their phones were in service.

Now perhaps you are hoping for an additional miracle, that our friend Beauchamp could still be alive, eager to buy a new raincoat with which to battle the various elements. I'm sorry, Dear Reader, but we must bow before Reality and admit that even the best of mystical detectives must uncoil from the weirdness that is the Kingdom of Florida.

Chapter 88

That November, Joan and Mia were sitting at a round table in the heart of West Palm Beach, sipping coffee near the public fountains, watching children frolic among orchestrated geysers of colorful light.

"Your haircut is perfect, Mia."

"Really? It's not too short? It's not overly trying to be smart?"

"It's just right," Joan assured her. "Short and sweet—and very intelligent."

Smiling, Mia returned the compliment. "I like your shirt, Joan. So blue and feathery. Makes me think of a heron."

"Found it at a thrift store."

"Nice. And your hair is getting so long. And thick. Wow, Joan. Very thick."

"Yeah, it's a tangled mess."

"No, it looks great. For real."

Joan shrugged. "Thanks. So, tell me about your recovery, Mia. I'm sorry I left town all of a sudden. I hope you understand."

"I understand why you left. So many false accusations. Seriously, what was up with that witchcraft thing? Crazy."

"Yeah," Joan said, sighing. "They said I used magic to blow up the military base. Even after the investigation was dropped, I was getting harassed."

"I tried to defend you. I even used Aristotelian logic to prove your innocence, but nobody would listen to reason. Everyone just wanted to burn you."

A wave of high-pitched voices hit the air as if to destroy it, or perhaps to recreate it in the image of children. "Hush," a parent scolded, "not so loud." But the hushing was followed by more gushing joy, because what is more wonderful to a group of children than water and sunlight and music?

"Show me your foot," Joan said. "I want to see how it healed."

"It's pretty legit," Mia said, taking a deep breath. "I still have some pain, and sometimes I limp. But look." She slipped off her sandal. "Five whole toes! All in a row!"

"Nice."

"Yeah, you can see my foot is covered with scars, but that's okay. My physical therapist says I can do anything now. Hiking, running, politics."

The music fueling the fountain picked up another beat, the pulsing streams of water rising toward the sky, making the children dance around with their arms in the air.

"They cancelled the Demon Dance this year," Mia said. "I guess the creeps who organized it are all gone."

"Good riddance. They can't hurt girls like Donna anymore. They can't abuse anyone or anything on earth, ever again."

Sipping their coffees, the women tried not to gloat, although they were aware that they'd helped bring down the WINGS.

"How's life in Savannah?" Mia asked with an edge to her voice. "You don't do Facebook anymore, and you rarely answer your phone. What do you do all day? Just paint and make stained glass? I was surprised when I heard you were back for Thanksgiving. And I was shocked when you actually texted me."

"I'm sorry for how I've been, Mia. I just needed some space, and some time to figure out my life after we almost—"

"Died," Mia said. "We almost died."

Color spectrums filled the autumn air like leaves on invisible trees, the tropical fountains rising in a majesty of melody while the children continued their never-ending frolic.

"Mia, tell me about you and Rico. Any news?"

"Rico goes to Basic Training in two weeks. He's become so serious about fighting terrorism and stuff. We're getting along, and we'll try to stay together."

"Good. I'm happy for you."

"Anyway, I'm heading to Harvard next semester. I've been taking online courses."

"Do you like those?"

"I really do, especially my business class. I think I understand economics. Given enough capital, I could invest wisely and buy up the whole world."

"Oh dear," Joan said, smiling nervously.

Mia laughed. "Don't freak out. I'll probably just end up as President of the United States."

"Oh, that's good."

"Yeah, and speaking of good. Check this out." She pointed across the sparkling fountains where two handsome guys appeared like angels, strutting through mist toward the table.

"Hey," the guys said, monosyllabically cool. And of course they weren't angels but Rico and Dontey in all their glory, one like a beach bum and the other a preppy athlete.

"Hey!" Mia shouted, almost spilling her coffee. "What a nice surprise! Rico, you turd! You said you couldn't get away from your family today."

"I used some evasive maneuvers," he said, and then stared like someone seeing a ghost. "Hey, Joan. Look at you."

"Yeah," Dontey said, "look at you, Joan. Stylin' with long black hair. What happened to the purple?"

Not wanting to discuss fashion with the guys, the happy artist turned her attention to a higher calling. "Anybody hungry?"

"Heck yeah," Dontey said, even though he was full of turkey and mashed potatoes. "I could go for a smoothie."

Joan shook her head. "Not a smoothie. I was thinking about a milkshake."

"A milkshake?" Dontey contemplated for a moment. "Yeah, that sounds good."

"Or not," Rico said, flexing his abs. "I'm hankering for some oatmeal."

"Hankering for oatmeal?" Dontey burst out laughing. "Really? Oatmeal?"

"Dude, I'm in training for Basic Training. I'm loading up on good carbs and avoiding sugar. I mean, avoiding most sugar." He leaned down to kiss Mia. It was a rather long kiss, and feel free, Dear Reader, to holler, "GROSS!"

Mia ended the kiss by playfully punching Rico in the stomach. "We want milkshakes. And we want them now."

"Oatmeal is for lovers," Rico said, leaning in for another kiss.

"GROSS!" half the universe seemed to cry, while the other half of the universe whispered, "Aww, that's sweet."

"As long as we're talking food," Dontey said, "I'm all about ice cream. The coach says I can eat all the ice cream I want—if we keep winning."

"Didn't you lose the game last week?" Rico asked.

"They won, forty to six," Joan answered. "I saw the video highlights. Dontey rushed for a hundred yards and three touchdowns."

Rico slapped him on the shoulder. "You da man! And you da Hercules!"

"Ouch," Dontey replied.

"Well," Joan said, a little impatiently, "we could stay here all day and watch you guys entertain us. Or—"

"We could get milkshakes," Mia said, "and entertain our tummies."

"I vote milkshakes." Dontey pointed across the street toward a popular place called Melting in Paradise.

"No, not there," Joan said. She stood up from the table. "We know who serves the best elixirs in the world."

Mia whispered, "Are you serious?"

"Are you serious?" Rico echoed.

Feeling queasy, Dontey asked, "Joan, are you talking about the place that serves monster? I mean, monstera?"

"Yeah, that's the place."

"You're crazy," Dontey said. "You want to travel back down to the Everglades?"

Joan smiled. "How's the church van running?"

Dontey paused before replying. "It has lots of dents and scratches and rust. And it smells a bit funky."

"And?"

"Yeah, it's running pretty good."

"Perfect," Joan said. She raised her arms to feel the wind beneath the royal palms, her feathery blouse shimmering like a bird about to take flight.

"No," Mia said. "Absolutely not. Let's just stay here and hang out. Let's just settle for some ice cream and oatmeal."

Those words put Rico in a difficult position because a good boyfriend should agree with everything that his girlfriend says and answer her whims with the ancient formula for relationship success: "You're right, babe." However, he accidentally blurted out, "A road trip does sound better than oatmeal."

To which Mia replied, "Rico, you're such a turd. Dontey, speak reason to him, will you?"

"I don't know," Dontey said, wishing he didn't have to take sides. He thought it would be better for everyone, especially for Joan, to avoid the wilderness and stay downtown with its nice park and cornucopia of stores. The Everglades were so unpredictable, and who knows what sort of trauma might be resurrected by getting too close to the river of death. He cleared his throat. "After everything that happened down there, can we risk it again?"

Before anyone could reply, a barefoot child careened toward the table, slipping and sliding and yelling with delight, taking a detour from the fountains. Mia noticed that the little girl was rollicking around with a foot that had a deformed toe, the merest of stubs, and yet she played without fear.

"Careful, kiddo," Mia said, reaching out to offer support.

"Ha!" the child replied, leaping back toward the mystical game in the colorful mist. "Ha!"

Mia was able to discern an intelligent answer when she heard one, and, being a genius, she immediately changed her mind about heading south. "Okay, let's go on a stupid road trip. But not too close to any form of invasive reptile. I think we should go explore that castle made of coral, you know, Coral Castle. They say it's very romantic, and sort of eerie."

Dontey slapped Rico on the shoulder. "Sort of eerie. Just like you."

"Oh yeah?" the soldier-in-training said, assuming a kung fu stance. "You want to mess with me? C'mon, dude. You want some kung? Or some fu?"

It was an old joke, but Dontey responded with the words that everyone loves to say. "Oh, bring me some fu, bro. Bring me some fu."

Joan interrupted the comic battle of alpha males with a serious and practical question. "Where's the van?"

"The van? It's over there," Dontey said. He pointed beyond the fountains at the glowing vehicle parked in front of a hearse.

Joan grinned, her face fluttering with light. She knew this trip to the castle would be epic, like a medieval adventure, a dazzling quest, a holy pilgrimage, and therefore quite dangerous. There'd be time-travelers, angels, illuminati, two-headed goats, treasure, Russians, gloom, doom, and fantastical redemption.

"Give me the keys," Joan of the Everglades said. "I'll get us there."

THE END

Made in the USA
Lexington, KY
16 June 2017